THE HOLLYWOOD  MURDER MYSTERIES

BOOK
TWENTY
1966

THE CASE
OF THE SHAGGY
STALKER

PETER S. FISCHER

www.petersfischer.com

The Case of the Shaggy Stalker
Copyright © 2018 by Peter S. Fischer All rights reserved.
Except as permitted under the U.S. Copyright Act of 1976, no part
of this publication may be reproduced, distributed or transmitted
in any form or by any means, nor stored in a database or retrieval
system, without prior written permission of the publisher. The
characters and events in this book are fictitious. Any similarity
to persons living or dead is coincidental and not intended by the
author. However certain events and passages, including dialogue,
may involve celebrities well known to the public in the year 1963.
All of these are fictional as well.

ISBN 978-0-9998846-0-7

To my grandson, Peter—
The Happy Wanderer

CHAPTER ONE

It was two years ago when I first met Walter Mirisch. It was some sort of Academy event and we found ourselves sitting at a table for eight. He was on his own that night and so was I. In an industry crawling with egotistical self-aggrandizing charlatans, Walter is an anomaly. Warm and friendly, polite to a fault, possessed of a pixie-like sense of humor, I seriously doubt that he has an enemy in the world, quite an achievement in a business where often success can be measured by how many of your competitors' scalps you can hang on your wall. And now here I am on this warm August afternoon being ushered into the private office of this industry icon who has produced dozens of top notch films, many of them classics, and who now has made the foolhardy decision to option my best-selling novel, 'Malibu at Midnight', the first featuring my dashing protagonist Sam August, a Yankee version, if you will, of Ian Fleming's James Bond.

Walter, a slim man and not tall, shakes my hand warmly, offers coffee, and I accept. He reiterates that he is looking forward to filming 'Malibu', but sorry to say—and here his face falls—we will have to get along without Robert Redford who is committed to Arthur Penn's 'The Chase' with Brando. After that Redford's Broadway contract has locked him into the screen version of 'Barefoot in the

Park'. Mirisch is unwilling to wait for well over a year and I don't blame him.

"I have a suggestion," he says to me, "and I think this gentleman would be excellent in the part but I won't sign him without your approval. There are those in the community who believe the young man is a pretty boy who can't act. I disagree."

"Who are we talking about, Walter?"

"Bob Wagner."

I feel a fist clench in my gut. I am one of those in the community who believes that Wagner is a lightweight nonentity. Walter reads my face.

"Before you say anything, there's a piece of film I want you to look at. Jack Smight sent it over when he heard we couldn't get Redford. Jack's filming 'Harper', the new Paul Newman picture over at Warners, and he tells me Wagner is a revelation. Come on next door. I want to run a scene for you."

Hiding my disappointment I follow Walter into the adjoining office where a screen and projector have been set up. He signals to the projectionist. The lights dim. The film rolls.

Newman and Wagner share the scene and Newman is ragging on Wagner something fierce, trying to provoke a visceral reaction. The woman you love is weak, Newman yells at him, untrustworthy, a low life drug addict. We both know she's a worthless junkie, he goes on, nothing more than human debris. You can see Wagner becoming more and more distraught even though he is holding a gun on Newman. And then Wagner's emotions betray him and he starts to cry, not man-made glycerine drops but the real thing and I can't take my eyes off him.

The lights come up. I look over at Walter who gives me a querying look.

"Okay by me," I say and Walter smiles.

"I thought you might say that, Joe," Walter says. "Wagner's

manager is really hot for the project and as for Wagner, he loves the character and he loves the book. His only reservations are the script which has yet to be written and the extent of your participation. He'd like a meet-and-greet and I assured him that was no problem."

"Sure."

"They're shooting today at Warner's Stage 12."

"I know the way, Walter," I smile. I should. The first seven years of my career were spent on the Warner's lot in Burbank, flakking it's pictures, the good, the average and the mediocre. We never made any 'bad' pictures. I know because Jack Warner told me so.

I head over to the San Fernando Valley where the Warner Bros. studio is located, first making a phone call to Bunny to break a lunch date.

"No problem, Joe,' she says. "I'm up to my tuckus in research for an expose we're doing on PG&E," she says.

"What are they up to now?" I ask.

"The usual," she says. "How'd your meeting go with whats-his-name?"

One of my wife Bunny's failings is that she has a near-zero knowledge of the business side of the movie industry.

"Mirisch, cute face. Walter Mirisch. Shall I spell it for you, or maybe you'd like a list of his movies like 'The Apartment' and 'Some Like it Hot' and 'The Great Escape'—

"Okay, okay," she says. "I give up."

"The meeting went great and I'll tell you all about it over supper."

"Can't wait," she says and hangs up.

I get in my car and head for the studio. I slip out of my jacket and toss it on the passenger seat, then turn up the air conditioning to full blast. It is the end of August and we have had four straight days of 90+ temperatures, more expected. When I turn off Barham Boulevard into the main gate, there is an unfamiliar face peering out at me from the security shack. He recognizes neither me nor my beloved vintage Bentley but as my name is on his clipboard he is forced to let me pass. How things have changed in the intervening years since I first went to work for Jack Warner when, on my first week on payroll eighteen years ago, I was sent to Mexico to rescue Humphrey Bogart from the federales. No, I don't need directions to Stage 12, I tell the gate guard with a straight face. Actually many years ago I was born here in the back of the dispensary, I say, and one of these days Mr. Warner is going to acknowledge me. Pray it happens soon, I'm not getting any younger. And so I drive off into the maze of offices and sound stages leaving the newbie guard gazing after me scratching his head.

I get lucky. I find a parking spot alongside Stage 13. I get out of the car and slip my CLERGY card onto the windshield visor. Not that it means anything here on the lot, I use it out of habit and I am positive it has saved me countless tow-aways. I dart across the street, avoiding a bullet-riddled Ford from the Thirties, and look up as she emerges from the door to Stage 12. As gorgeous as ever, Lauren Bacall at 42 is just as breathtaking as she was in 1944 when Bogey made her his child bride.

"Betty!" I call out.

She hesitates at the top of the steps, squints in my direction and then grins broadly.

"Joe!"

"Tis me, fair lady," I say.

She hurries down the steps, I hurry to her and we embrace like long lost Shriners who haven't seen each other since the last parade.

"My God, you look great. What's your secret ?" she asks.

"Dissolute living," I reply. "Obviously you're into it as well."

I have known Betty Bacall for years, ever since I worked with Bogie on 'Sierra Madre' and anyone who calls her 'Lauren' doesn't know her at all. The three of us became close and I was one of the few permitted to visit Bogie at his home a month before he died of

8

cancer in '57. After that Betty and I kind of lost track but here she is, as if the intervening years had never happened.

"How's everything?" I ask.

"Passable," she replies flatly.

"And number two?"

"We're a threesome. Me, Jason and Johnnie Walker."

Rumors abound that her second marriage to Jason Robards Jr. has not been going well. She's just confirmed why.

"Sorry to hear it."

"Life goes on," she shrugs. "Say, I hope you're not back here to peddle more pap for dear old Jack. You were much too good for him, Joe. Anyway, I love your books. You've cost me a lot of sleep."

"For which I apologize. No, I'm here on business." She looks at me curiously. "Robert Wagner."

"Ah," she smiles. "Your Sam August character. Yes, R J. would be very good. Two of my favorite people working together. Glorious."

"Could happen."

"Well, I believe he's in his dressing room. Left at the sound stage, second building on the right, first floor."

"Thanks," I say with a wink and a smile.

"If you need help convincing the guy, which I doubt, talk to Paul. They are practically blood brothers and by the way, Paul loved your book as much as I did."

Paul Newman loved my book? Wow. If only he were a few years younger, he'd be perfect for— well, never mind.

"Joanne loves R.J., too. You know, they did a film together about ten years ago—". Joanne Woodward is Newman's wife. They've been married for ages.

"'A Kiss Before Dying'," I say. "I saw it. He played a real son of a bitch."

"Indeed he did," Bacall replies.

I start off, then turn as she calls my name.

"Joe, you have heard about Jack." A statement, not a question. I turn back to her, alarmed.

"Jack Warner? What about him?" I frown.

She reads my mind. "Sorry to scare you. No, he's not dying, not yet at least, but rumors are flying, Joe. They say he's getting ready to quit."

"Never," I say.

"It's all over town. I was sure you knew."

"First I've heard of it."

"It won't be the same without the old bastard," Bacall says. "I'll actually be sorry to see him go."

"Sometimes rumors are just rumors, Betty. If I learn anything, I'll get back to you," I say.

"Do," she smiles and with a little wave, she walks off.

I head down the street mentally shaking my head. Jack Warner quitting the movie business? That's like Santa turning his back on Christmas. I make a note to drop in on the old tiger before I leave the lot.

I start off again but I don't get far because, as I turn the corner, here is my quarry coming toward me. At his side is a guy about his size wearing shades and a cowboy hat.

"Mr. Wagner," I say as he draws close.

A moment's hesitation and then a warm smile.

"You'd be Joe," he says.

"I would be," I say.

"Walter Mirisch called to say you'd be dropping by."

My attention is drawn to his companion. I look past the sunglasses and the Stetson and I recognize him. But before I can say anything, he puts out his mitt with an 'aw, shucks' smile.

"Ben Boxer, Mr. Bernardi. I'm Mr. Wagner's stand-in. Pleased to meet you."

Hah. If he's Ben Boxer, then I'm Humpty Dumpty. And if he's

pleased to meet me, how come he called me by name when Wagner hadn't used it. I fix him with a stare and let it go, at least for the moment.

"You'd better run on ahead, Ben. They're lighting scene 113. I'll be by shortly," Wagner says.

"Right, R.J.," Ben Boxer says. He breaks into a jog and hurries off. A star's stand-in does just that, he 'stands in' for the star while the Director of Photography and the gaffer arrange the lights for the next scene. As opposed to a stunt double who risks life and limb making the boss look like a stalwart hero in an action scene, a stand-in is a sedentary slug. Wagner and I continue toward the sound stage at a slower pace.

"I guess Mr. Mirisch told you how much I loved your book, Mr. Bernardi."

"He did and it's Joe."

"Joe. Right. I'm Bob or R.J., either one will do."

"Absolutely, Bob," I reply.

"So, about the screenplay. I assume you're going to write it, Joe."

"Not if I can help it. I write novels, not movies."

"Bullshit," he grins. "I saw 'Wildcatters' and it was terrific. The Academy screwed you out of an Oscar."

"Kind of you to say so."

"No way. Kindness I save for my cat. You get the straight goods." We arrive at Stage 12. "Look, Joe, the shooting schedule is all screwed up today and I'm going to be on call until at least four o'clock. How about drinks at the Smoke House around five?"

"Sure. See you then," I say as I shake his hand.

"This is going to be fun," he smiles but I see beyond it, something in his eyes that tells me this man has a lot on his mind.

"You bet," I say and head for my car as he jogs up the steps into the sound stage.

I slip behind the wheel and for a minute or two, I'm deep in thought. I'm bothered by something but I don't know what. Years ago I might have succumbed to paranoia but at 46 I've been there, done that, and amassed enough money to place a down payment on the Golden Gate Bridge. Is Wagner setting me up for a list of impossible demands? I doubt it. He has a reputation as a straight shooter, even tempered and lacking an oversized ego. Something else is amiss and I guess in a few hours I'll find out what it is.

Just then the man who calls himself Ben Boxer emerges from the stage and heads down the street in the direction of the commissary. I hop out of the car and jog after him.

"Gunnar! Wait up!" I shout and he turns at the sound of his name. A rookie mistake. I should call him on it but probably won't. Gunnar Larsen is a private detective who works for Cosmo Stryker who is a very good friend of my very good friend, Mick Clausen, a successful bail bondsman who is married to my ex-wife Lydia.

"Nice disguise," I say as I reach him. "It wouldn't fool a blind turtle."

"I'm sorry but I—"

"Yeah, yeah, I know. You have no idea who I am even though you've been to my house twice guzzling my Smirnoff's. You know, Gunnar, whenever I'm told you're coming, I have to water the vodka, just to stay even."

His face lights up.

"Mr. Bernardi. Sorry I didn't recognize you."

"That's because you're sober, Gunnar. So what's going on? What are you doing in Bob Wagner's hip pocket?"

"Can't help you, Mr. Bernardi. I'm on the job."

He's handing me the old p.i./client confidentially gag which legally doesn't exist. It keeps popping up in Jack Warner movies but truth be told, most private eyes would sell out their clients for a bottle of beer.

"Okay, how about if I rat you out to Mr. Wagner?"

"I have no problem with that," Gunnar says.

"Aha," says I, "which means you're working for him."

"Like I say, Mr. Bernardi, I'm not at liberty to talk but I have no problem with you speaking to Mr. Wagner," he says once again.

I say I will and I do.

CHAPTER TWO

The tourists don't know about The Smoke House. Good thing. It remains a refuge of privacy for show business celebrities, away from the insistent intrusions of fans, young and old, and their ubiquitous autograph books. Located immediately next door to the Warner Bros. lot, it is best described as a roadhouse restaurant which is frequented daily by executives, actors and other notables from Warners and nearby Universal from eleven in the morning until past eleven at night. The food is excellent, the bar well stocked and the staff pleasant and accommodating.

I arrive promptly at four, pull up a stool at the bar and order a Coors. I expect Wagner to be late because filming is an unpredictable exercise but he surprises me when he walks in at ten past, the faux Ben Boxer at his side. Wagner whispers something into Boxer's ear. Boxer nods and slips onto a stool at the end of the bar. Wagner approaches with a smile grabbing me by the elbow and suggesting we might be more comfortable at a booth near a window.

As we settle in, he says, "I'm having impure thoughts about Pamela Tiffin. Marian would not approve." Tiffin's his nubile teenage co-star.

"I know the feeling," I say. He has been married to actress Marian Marshall for three years after the breakup of his celebrated marriage to Natalie Wood. Those who know say it's a good marriage and he's a good father to Marshall's two sons from her previous marriage to director Stanley Donen.

Just then raven-haired Sophie, a fixture of many years, comes by to take our order. Me, Coors. Bob, scotch on the rocks. I lean back and watch as he digs into the bowl of peanuts.

"Let's talk about the book," he says.

"I'd rather talk about Ben Boxer," I say.

He looks at me with a guileless little boy expression.

"Sorry. What about him?"

I shake my head disapprovingly.

"We're getting off on the wrong foot here, Bob. The guy's name is Gunnar Larsen. He's a top of the line private detective in the employ of Cosmo Stryker and he doesn't come cheap. You know it and I know it so why don't you ease my mind and tell me about it?"

Wagner hesitates, smiling.

"No offense but I'm not sure it's any of your business, Joe."

"I think it is. Walter and I have a lot riding on this film. Not just the money involved but I am very protective of Sam August. He's like a member of my family and I don't want anything to spoil this venture. Whatever is going on, it's obviously very serious, and maybe you're right, maybe it is none of my business but if there is the slightest chance it jeopardizes the film we either talk about it or part ways now. Your call."

At that moment Sophie returns with our drinks. Wagner doesn't take his eyes off me and he doesn't speak until she is out of earshot.

"It's a family matter. Nothing you need to worry about."

"I'd rather judge that for myself," I say.

"You'll just have to trust me," he replies.

"I'd like to. I can't," I reply as I get to my feet, leaving my beer untouched and putting out my hand. "Sorry this didn't work out. I'll explain it to Walter."

Wagner ignores my outstretched hand.

"Maybe some other time," he says.

"Maybe so," I smile, then turn on my heel and walk out.

As I head for my car, I'm troubled. Wagner is a successful actor, well off, but far from a rich man and certainly not in a position to refuse a starring role in a movie to be produced by Walter Mirisch and a career that could rival Sean Connery's. Whatever his problem is, it's obvious it is major. It's also obvious he is going to keep it to himself.

"It's not going to work out," I say to Walter when I get him on the phone.

"What happened?"

"Damned if I know," I say. "He has a major personal problem and he's keeping it to himself, even if it means passing on this opportunity. Any other thoughts?"

"None as good as Wagner," Walter says. "I'll get my casting people on it. Maybe we overlooked someone."

"Get back to me."

"I will," he says and hangs up.

It's Tuesday. Family night out for the Bernardis. It used to be Biff's All-American Diner when Yvette was a tot but now that she is a grown up young lady of twelve, she has discovered Bella's Ristorante, a few blocks from the house. Correction. She has discovered Bella's seventeen year old son Pietro, dark haired and blue-eyed and possessed of Frankie Avalon's charm and good looks. She fancies that she is learning Italian and has worked herself up to 'Grazie' and 'Prego' and a dozen pasta dishes. She makes sure we sit where Pietro is waiting table and then spends a couple of hours pretending not to notice him while he flirts with her outrageously looking for a decent sized tip. Bunny is highly amused by all this. I merely wonder what this oily lech has in mind for her. The world is beginning to become more than I can handle. At 46 I am turning into a geezer.

My gaze looks past Pietro, his smile and his order pad, and settles on the television set above the bar. I frown as I see police cars, an ambulance, a shot of Mt. Sinai Hospital and then a file photo of Bob Wagner. I get up quickly, excusing myself and hurrying to the bar.

"What's going on, Chuck?" I ask the bartender indicating the TV set.

"Looks like a hit and run."

"Wagner?"

"His wife."

"She okay?"

"They're not saying. She was at a local sports arena picking up her two kids and apparently this guy comes like a bat out of hell from nowhere and plows into her as she and the kids and some guy were crossing the street to her car."

"Some guy?"

He shrugs."Some guy. What do I know?"

"Thanks, Pete," I say and hurry back to the table where I slide a fifty underneath the salt and pepper shakers.

"Gotta go, honey," I say, leaning in and giving Bunny a kiss.

"What's going on?" she asks. I tell her. "And what has Robert Wagner got to do with you? I thought he turned down the part."

"He did, but that was five hours ago," I say.

I lean in to kiss Yvette goodbye but she backs off, screwing up her face. "Dad!" she whines, much too old for a public display of affection with a parent. I tousle her hair instead. "Be good to Bunny," I tell her and hurry away.

Traffic on Beverly Boulevard is light and in a matter of minutes, I find myself in Mt. Sinai's parking lot. Given Wagner's celebrity status I know I'm going to be stonewalled by the reception desk so I make for the emergency entrance where I get lucky. I don't see Wagner anywhere but I do spot Cosmo Stryker leaning over the waiting room water cooler filling one of those miniscule paper cups.

"So, Cosmo," I say, "what the hell happened out there?"

He looks up and smiles.

"Hey, Joe. Good to see you, pal. Been a while."

"Never mind the eyewash, my friend, what happened to Wagner's wife? Your guy was looking the wrong way? What?"

His look is innocence.

"Sorry, Joe, I don't know what—"

"You don't know what I'm talking about. Cosmo, just because I write for the movies doesn't mean I'm a complete idiot. I ran into Gunnar Larsen earlier today. He was running interference for Bob Wagner using an alias. I assume one of your guys was doing the same for his wife."

The smile doesn't leave Cosmo's face, it merely turns to ice and his eyes shrink to razor-wide slits on each side of his nose.

"You're looking through the wrong keyhole, Joe, but even if you weren't, I couldn't talk to you about it. Confidentiality privilege."

Now where have I heard that before?

"I understand completely," I say. "I would never suggest you betray a client. So how have you got it set up? Six guys, two on Wagner, two on the wife and two on the kids, around the clock? Sure, it would have to be, otherwise it doesn't work."

"Nice seeing you, Joe," Cosmo says coldly as he brushes past me. I turn to follow him but just then Wagner appears from the bowels of the emergency ward. He stops short when he sees me, takes in Cosmo, puts it together. His expression is more one of surprise than anger and he quickly forces a smile as he approaches me.

"You and Cosmo have been talking," he says.

"Cosmo and I go back a dozen years, Bob. He's an old friend, and no, he didn't rat you out."

Wagner hesitates. "Maybe you and I should talk," he says.

"First, how's your wife?" I ask.

"Sedated and sleeping. She'll be staying the night for observation but everything looks good. Scrapes and bruises, nothing more."

"The apple pie here is terrific. So's the coffee," I say, taking his arm and starting to lead him toward the hospital cafeteria. He shrugs me off.

"I'll get the boys and meet you there."

"Who's watching Marian?" I ask.

"Jacoby."

I nod appreciatively. Mike Jacoby. Cosmo's top guy.

"Nothing but the best," I observe.

"So I've been told," Wagner replies.

I've just slathered vanilla ice cream atop my apple pie when I spot Wagner in the doorway with two young boys. I wave them over and am introduced to Peter, 13, and Joshua, 11, Marian Wagner's sons from her prior marriage to director Stanley Donen. Surprisingly they are not sullen or surly and they actually look me in the eye when we speak. At Bob's invitation they race off to the dessert section as Bob pulls up a chair.

"Your wife still resting?"

"As best she can. We chatted earlier. She has no idea what happened. She never saw it coming."

"And Jacoby?"

"Him either."

"You planning to eat? You probably should."

"Maybe later."

We sit in silence for a few moments. I decide to wait him out.

"I suppose Walter's checking availabilities," Wagner says. I nod. "I hear Charlie Bronson's available."

"I hope not," I deadpan.

"Seriously, Joe, I want to do this but if it doesn't work out, you could do a lot worse than Warren Beatty."

"He's committed to Arthur Penn for some 1930's gangster picture.

Not that we were that interested. We weren't."

"Cliff Robertson?"

"Too old."

"George Hamilton?"

"We need someone who can throw a punch, not a party," I say. We continue in silence.

"Maybe it was just an accident," I say. "Guy panics, runs for it."

Wagner gives me a look that would freeze a tiki torch. Finally he speaks.

"We've been getting anonymous letters slipped under the front door in the dead of night. Threats. Ugly threats. Also phone calls at all times of the day or night. We're set up to trace the calls but he never stays on more than twenty seconds. His voice is muffled, disguised. Marian's his target but he has plenty of venom left over for me. I hired Cosmo over a week ago. I think he's doing a good job but this pervert, whoever he is, is not giving up."

"No idea who it is?"

"No."

"Police?"

"Not involved. Police means the press in your face twenty-four hours a day and this kind of publicity I don't need." He hesitates. "I've been involved with a lot of women in my time, Joe. Most were unattached. A few were married, unhappily, to real jerks."

"Jerk or not, a jealous husband?"

"I really don't think so. I started behaving myself when I married Natalie. If it's a husband it's from way back and why is he showing up now?" He falls silent. "Marian has a notion but it's gone nowhere." I wait. "She's only guessing."

"Okay, she's guessing," I say and wait for more.

"His name is Horatio Cummings, mid-40s, effete, a third rate hack writer of romance novels. They met in London years ago when she was married to Stanley Donen. Stanley was directing

'Indiscreet' with Grant and Bergman and at some damned party at some damned manor house outside the city we were introduced to this guy. For some reason Cummings fixated on Marian, sending her flowers, inviting her to lunch knowing that Stanley was busy but forgetting that she had two boys to take care of. He planned to write one of his silly novels with a fictionalized Marian as the heroine. Finally, when he wouldn't take no for an answer, she told Stanley and he went after Cummings with a gun. Cummings must have been tipped Stanley was on his way because he abandoned his flat and fled the city. Bottom line, he hasn't been heard from since."

"Until now?"

"Hard to believe after all this time," Wagner says, then looks past my shoulder. "Let's talk about the Dodgers. Here come the boys."

Peter and Joshua approach the table, smiling broadly, partly because of the chocolate brownies they are carrying but mostly, I suspect, because they know their mother is resting comfortably and is going to be alright.

"Looks good," I say.

"You bet," Peter replies.

"You two guys must have had a heck of a fright out there on the street," I say.

"Nah," Peter says with false bravado.

"Me either," Joshua chimes in. "Santa Claus," he adds.

"What? What about Santa Claus?" Bob asks.

"He looked just like Santa Claus. White hair and a white beard but mean looking."

"Josh thinks he saw the guy," Peter says.

"I did," Joshua insists.

"Did not. You were curled up on the pavement just like me."

"Whoa. Take it easy, guys," Bob says. "Now Josh, no kidding around. Don't say you saw the driver of the car if you didn't. This is very serious."

"I saw him. Saw him before, too."

"Before?" Wagner shoots me a puzzled look.

"A couple of days ago. I was shooting hoops in the driveway and he drove by the house a couple of times and he was always slowing down to look at me and then driving away."

"What kind of a car was it, Josh?" I ask.

"I don't know much about cars," the boy says. "It was white, kind of old looking."

"Two doors? Four doors?" I ask.

"I don't remember."

"Jacoby says he saw the car driving away. Got a partial tag. SAR something," Bob says. "He thought it was a light grey."

So much for a possible accident, I think to myself. Attempted murder has raised its ugly head.

We chat a while longer, avoiding any further talk of a deliberate attempt on Marian Wagner's life. Just as Bob and the boys are getting ready to go check on Marian and I am going to catch up with Bunny and Yvette, I hear the wail of sirens in distance, approaching. The sound cuts out and I peer out a window that overlooks the emergency entrance. An ambulance pulls in followed by a squad car which in turn is followed by an unmarked civilian car. We start to step into the emergency area but are blocked off as two gurneys are wheeled in followed by two uniformed cops. Staffers immediately jump into action. I hear the words 'code blue' and 'armed robbery', 'blood loss', and 'OR stat'. The first of the two men is covered with blood and a technician is holding an IV bag aloft. The second also suffers from an apparent GSW and is moaning pitifully as a nurse, running beside the gurney, presses down hard on his chest area. Then I look back and spot Lou Cioffi, the dynamo crime reporter for the *L.A. Times*, hot on the trail of a story. As he passes by he spots me and then takes in Bob Wagner, back to me with a puzzled look and then continues chasing the second gurney.

When he gets to the doors to the operating room, a beefy orderly prevents him from entering. At that moment Bob and the boys head out for Marian and I skedaddle for the exit. I have no interest in getting into a protracted conversation with Lou about my presence in a hospital emergency ward with Robert Wagner.

CHAPTER THREE

Wednesday morning. Bunny tried to wake me twice. I rolled over, burying myself in the covers. She didn't try a third time and by the time I actually consider joining the world, it's a few minutes to ten. I spent a fitful night dreaming about hit-and-runs and white sedans and Bob Wagner whom I was chasing down ill-lit corridors and back alleys. I never did catch up with him. Freud would have loved it.

Just before nine last evening Walter had called with a brainstorm. Had I heard of an actor named Clint Eastwood? I said I had. Mysterious, taciturn, star of three spaghetti westerns helmed by Sergio Leone, Walter thought he might be right for Sam. I disagreed. Though no James Bond, Sam August is a quick man with a quip and catnip for the ladies. I see none of that in Eastwood who seems to make a career of avoiding dialogue. He'll probably make a pretty durable star of western programmers some day but that's about it. Walter disagrees but I have final say. Someday he'll thank me for not letting him make a big mistake.

By the time I eat breakfast and make my way to my second floor office, hot mug of coffee in hand, it's nearly eleven. I've already pored over my two must-reads in the *L.A. Times*. Phineas has written a rave for 'Dr. Zhivago' and insists that Omar Sharif be presented with the Oscar. I don't go that far but I agree that it is a marvelous film. Lou Cioffi's crime story leads the Metro section and covers a liquor store holdup on Western Avenue. A brain dead junkie high on meth walked in, demanding money and waving a .38 caliber revolver. The owner reached under the counter and pulled out a pump-action shotgun. Both fired simultaneously. The store owner is surviving minor injuries. The body of the junkie is lying in the morgue waiting for 'someone with a heavy duty trash bag to come and claim him.' At times Lou has a way with words that exceed good taste. Acidly accurate but hardly politic. Happily there is no mention of me or Bob Wagner.

I place a call to my agent Barry Loeb, all-knowing all-seeing expert on the vagaries of the publishing business. He bounces onto the phone as only he can, all smiles and optimism. The original can-do kid.

"The publisher loves the new manuscript," he tells me joyfully. "They're looking at a hundred thousand initial press run."

"I've heard that song before, amigo. Tell 'em I'll settle for fifty."

"Good luck. Actually, by the time they're ready to push the go-button, it'll be down to twenty."

"It always is," I say ruefully. "So, my brilliant compadre, I need your help."

"Shoot."

"Horatio Cummings."

"British, fiftyish. Writes women's weepies, years ago sold a lot, can't write worth a lick, probably thinks Jack London was once the prime minister of England."

"You know him?"

"Know of him," Barry replies.

"Where is he?"

"Career wise? South of nowhere."

"Geographically."

"No idea."

"But you could find out."

"Possibly."

"Then do it."

"What's the interest?"

"Hush, hush. You and me. Nobody else. When I can tell you, I will."

"Gotcha."

I hang up and reach behind me to the shelf on which sits my latest effort, 'The Ill Mannered Diplomat'. Last year's confection, "The Colorado Cabal" third in the series, is the one giving Barry delusions of prosperity. My publisher wouldn't order an initial printing of a hundred thousand for anything, not even Henry Miller with illustrations. On the other hand, their merchandising and promotion are first rate and they've turned Sam August into a household name. I can't complain.

I'm on page 54. The Bulgarian *chargé d'affaires* has the glamorous magazine editor, Dawn LaRue, trapped in his hotel suite while Sam twiddles his thumbs at Harry's Bar waiting for her to arrive for their dinner date at Maxim's. The phone rings. Less than an hour has passed. Barry is on the line.

"Horatio Cummings is still alive and still writing," he says.

"In London."

"Yes, but rumor has it he is here in Los Angeles writing a screenplay based on one of his novels. My source tells me he doesn't know which production company but it's certain to be a poverty row wannabe. Cummings wrote the book under a pseudonym which will be his screen credit if the thing ever goes to film."

"Name?"

"Wanda Periwinkle."

"Good God," I say. "But you didn't get the name of the

production company."

"Sorry. That she didn't know."

"She? Barry, are you into someone new?" I say, amused. Barry, diminutive though he may be, has a reputation about town as a prolific cocksman.

"Keep your filthy thoughts to yourself, Joe. Do you want me to pursue this or not?"

"No, I'll take it from there. Thanks, Barry. Great work as usual."

I set my book aside and pull a tome from one of the shelves. I am about to leaf through it when my phone rings. Normally I don't much like the phone. It rarely brings good news but without my precious Glenda Mae here to run interference, I'm helpless. I'm hoping it's either Walter or Barry and not some lecture director hoping to convince me to speak at the East Dry Hole, Wyoming's Literary Club, gratis, of course, and pay your own way to and from.

I pick up.

"I didn't know you were pals with Robert Wagner." I know the voice. My worst nightmare has come calling.

"Have been for years, Lou."

"Who knew?" Lou Cioffi laughs. "So how's his wife?"

"Fine, I guess."

"I'm talking about the hit and run, Joe. What do you know about it? I keep hearing that it might not have been accidental."

"Hearing from who?" I say with annoyance.

"Things I overheard at the hospital and then a couple of eye-witnesses when I went over to the sports center to check it out. So what's going on, Joe?"

"Nothing," I say. "I saw the coverage on the early evening news and drove over to see if I could be of help."

"For an old and dear friend."

"That's right."

Unlike Bob Wagner, Lou Cioffi really is an old and dear friend and a bulldog of a reporter. He can smell bullshit a hundred yards away and I have to be really careful lest he think I am hiding something. Which I am.

"Bob thinks it was some boozed up kid who just lost control of his car, nothing more than that," I say.

"Is that also what Mike Jacoby thinks?" replies Lou.

"Who?" I ask guilelessly.

"Mike Jacoby. One of Cosmo Stryker's top operatives. What's he doing helping Marian Wagner pick up the two kids from the sports center? Is she in trouble or is he? Cosmo doesn't come cheap nor do his guys."

"Honestly, Lou, I have no idea what you're talking about."

"Oh, Jesus," I hear him say. "Honestly, huh? Every time some mope starts out by telling me 'Honestly' I know I am about to buried in doggy dung. Come on, Joe, you're better than this. What's going on?"

"As far as I know, Lou, absolutely nothing but I tell you what, I'll talk to Bob and see if there's a problem. Maybe yes, maybe no, and if yes, maybe you can't print it. But either way I will get back to you."

"Can't ask for more than that," he says cheerily and hangs up. I hang up, too, and wipe my sweaty forehead with a Kleenex from the box on my desk. The last thing I need is for Lou to turn the Wagners into a front page story.

I turn my attention back to the ponderous book I had taken down from my shelf. Who's Who in World Literature is a pretty good source but I don't expect much. I'm not disappointed. Cummings rates two short paragraphs and a minuscule photo and I'm surprised to learn that before this Barbara Cartland impersonator turned to writing dreck, he was an award winning poet. Knowing as I do how little poets are paid for their work, I can hardly blame him for turning to the dark side.

With a sigh I return the book to the shelf. Lou Cioffi or no Lou Cioffi there are things I must do if I want to see Sam August come to life onscreen in the personna of Robert Wagner.

Next stop, my one-time secretary/Gal Friday whom I still miss after all these years. She continues to work at Bowles & Bernardi, the management firm that still bears my name. Bright and beautiful, she is a treasure and whatever I give her to do, she always gets it right. Glenda Mae Brown is one of a kind.

"What do you want?" she snarls into the phone.

I laugh as I always do. It's a game we play.

"I was calling to see if I could interest you in dinner at Scandia's, the Lakers game followed by two or three hours of wild and uninhibited sex."

"I'll take a raincheck on dinner, the rest of it you're on your own."

"Don't be smutty."

"Don't feed me straight lines," she says.

"I need a favor," I say.

"Don't you always."

"There's a guy in town. Horatio Cummings. He's using the alias Wanda Periwinkle."

"Get real."

"I kid you not. He's writing a screenplay from one of his books for some fifth-rate production company. I need to know which one and where I can find him and knowing as I do that you secretaries are an unofficial band of gossip-mongering sisters, I am pretty sure you can dig him up for me."

"You expect a lot."

"I do and the reward I just mentioned, dinner and then a Laker game, I will foot the bill for you and your husband Beau. The post game sex is up to you."

"I accept your generous offer, boss. Give me a couple of hours."

"I would give thee the moon and stars were it in my power,

beloved one, but two hours will do just fine."

"Yuck," she says, hanging up, obviously unimpressed by my poetic flight of fancy.

Two hours is not enough. I am trapped in the house waiting for her call, make a couple of notes for the new book, and eat a cheese sandwich while watching the latest episode of 'As The World Turns'. At quarter past two the phone rings. I pick up expectantly.

"What do you know about a guy named Garrison King?" Glenda Mae asks.

"Nothing."

"Regal King Productions?"

"Zero."

"That's where your boy/girl is camped out." She gives me an address on Western Avenue. I know the neighborhood. Rats fear it.

"Thanks, sweetheart. I won't forget this."

"Better not. Scandia and the Lakers are already on my to-do list."

By three o'clock I'm pulling into a parking lot opposite the address supplied by Glenda Mae. Pedro's Park-It is manned by a beefy Hispanic who I take to be Pedro. He sports long sideburns, a Pancho Villa mustache and carries a gun so I am confident my beloved Bentley is in good hands. Well it should be at a buck an hour, five dollar minimum.

The building is dingy, so is the second floor corridor and the glass-paned door to Regal King Productions needs a good washing. I take out my handkerchief and twist the doorknob to let myself in. The reception area is large enough to handle a wrap party but only if the picture is 'The Wizard of Oz' and only the munchkins are invited. The girl at the desk looks up in surprise at this sudden and unexpected invasion of her turf. She manages not to swallow her chewing gum.

"May I be of service?" she intones, pegging herself as a young lady bred and schooled in the San Fernando Valley.

"You're from the Valley," I say.

"Reseda. What's it to you?"

"I used to live in Burbank," I say.

"Break out the champagne," she says with a blasé shrug.

"I'm looking for Wanda," I say.

"Beg pardon."

"She also goes by Horatio Cummings, hiding out in men's suits."

"I do not know the person to whom you refer," she says archly.

I find this hysterically funny because on the far wall I spot a framed photo of a man who is most certainly Horatio Cummings in a filial embrace with another man who I assume to be Garrison King. Expensively dressed wearing a silk ascot and a diamond stick pin, he could easily win first runner up in a Wallace Beery looka-like contest.

"Sure you do," I say, "and I am not the IRS or Immigration and he doesn't owe me money."

She shakes her head.

"I'm sorry, sir, I can't help you. Perhaps Mr. King knows this person but he is presently out of the office. I could deliver a message, I am meeting him at six thirty at the Roosevelt Hotel."

I'll bet you are, I think to myself.

"That's very kind of you, Miss—uh—"

"Rosalie. Just Rosalie."

"Thank you, Rosalie. I'll check back with you in the morning."

"Who shall I say came by?" she asks.

"Faulkner. Bill Faulkner from Mississippi. I'm a writer."

"I'll tell him, Mr. Fawker," she smiles sweetly.

I can't wait to get out of there.

Once on the street, I find I have developed a thirst. I can either grab the car and go home or I can grab a Coors at a little cafe I have spotted at the end of the block. The sun is shining, the air is fresh and I see no sign of gang-bangers from Boyle Heights. I decide to chance it. It's when I get close that I realize what a brilliant decision I have made.

He's sitting at an outdoor table, hunched over, reading something I can't identify at this distance. His hair is long and white and tied together in a neat pony tail. His beard is minimal but white like his hair. Joshua Donen notwithstanding, he doesn't look a thing like Father Christmas, evil or otherwise. He's also the guy in the photo on Garrison King's wall as well as the "Who's Who".

I stop at his table and look down at him. He looks up at me curiously.

"I know you," I say.

"Really?" he responds."As far as I know I'm not wanted for anything. Maybe you're thinking of Monty Woolley."

"Horatio Cummings," I say.

"And just who the hell are you?"

"A devoted fan."

"Oh, so you're the guy," he says acidly.

"Flights of Wounded Starlings," I say.

"Oh, my God," he replies in disbelief.

"At university we studied neglected English poets. Your poem was my absolute favorite, Mr. Cummings. Mind if I sit down?"

He waves to an empty chair.

"As long as you don't start reciting."

I sit and note that he is reading Jackie Suzanne's 'Valley of the Dolls'. I take it this is research.

A waiter approaches and I order my Coors.

"You're a long way from home, Mr. Cummings," I observe.

"Movie work. I'm adapting a novel into a screenplay."

"Fascinating. What book? Maybe I know it."

"I doubt it. I didn't catch your name."

This is no time to be caught in a lie so I play it straight.

"Joe Bernardi."

I put out my hand. He looks at it, then back at me.

"Joe Bernardi. Sam August Joe Bernardi?"

"I am."

He shakes my hand.

"A pleasure."

"All mine. Where are you staying?"

"The Sportsman's Lodge. I would have preferred the Pink Palace but my producer is footing the bill and he is a notorious tightwad."

"We should have dinner together," I say. "I'll call you after I check my schedule."

"Don't call me, Mr. Bernardi. I'm registered under a nom de plume. Let me call you."

"Fine," I say, giving him my phone number. I get to my feet. "Perhaps tonight if you're not otherwise engaged."

"I'm a stranger in a strange land, Mr. Bernardi. Even so, tonight is spoken for but tomorrow evening would suit me just fine."

"Surely a man of your reputation must have friends here in Los Angeles."

"No, I'm reclusive by nature, even at my flat back in Belfast. I do not go out of my way to make new friends. You will be an exception.".

"I'm flattered," I say, giving him my card. "I'll be in touch." We shake and then I hustle off toward the parking lot. Next stop, the Sportsman's Lodge.

CHAPTER FOUR

The Sportsman's Lodge on Ventura Boulevard in Studio City is many miles from Hollywood and the major studios but its storied past is littered with the names of the great and the near great. Originally it was known as a trout farm inn where some of filmdom's biggest stars were known to hang out, stars like Tracy and Hepburn, Tallullah Bankhead, and Bette Davis. Clark Gable and John Wayne and Bogey taught their kids how to fish in the lake adjoining the premises. Another of those gems the tourists know little about.

I park a considerable distance from the front entrance in hopes of thwarting the 'ding devil'. I don't know for sure what he looks like but he has a habit of following me around, especially into parking lots where, unseen, he works his devilment on my unblemished Bentley. Hence, I now park wherever possible a considerable distance from other vehicles. Most of the time this ploy works.

I trudge to the front door and step inside. The desk clerk is sixty-ish and matronly and her name tag reads, 'Hi, I'm Matty, How May I Help You?'

"Checking in?" she asks with a smile. It's a nice smile. You can tell she was once a real looker before she was swamped by too many calories and too many years had gone by.

"No, but I'll bet you can help me," I say.

The smile doesn't fade but a curious look creeps into her eyes. "Mr. Bernardi?" she asks.

Taken aback, I give her a second look and that's when I recognize her.

"Tildy?"

She giggles and as she does she shimmies like a bowlful of Jello. "That's me," she replies.

Tilda Thayer, actual name Matilda Probst, was a third string ingenue in the early 1930's, getting thrown over by the likes of Ricardo Cortez, Buddy Rogers, and William Powell. In the '50s she slipped easily into character parts and then, like many others who never quite made it, disappeared into the Los Angeles landscape.

"Been a few years, Tildy," I say.

"Hadn't noticed," she says. "Too busy raising my grandchildren."

"Two? Three?"

"Seven, but who's counting? So, what can I do for you, Mr. B?"

"You have a guest, older man, white hair, wears it in a pony tail."

"Mr. Winkle," she says.

"Winkle?"

"Yes. Perry Winkle. I figure with a phony moniker like that he must be hiding from the cops. Or maybe a jealous husband?" she smiles with a wink.

"Wrong on both counts, Tildy, but I do have an abiding interest in what he's up to. Is he driving?"

"He is," she says, reaching for an index box and riffing through the cards until she finds the one she wants. "1964 Chevy Impala. Rented. I can tell from the plate number."

"Which is?

"SAR939."

"And the color?"

"Ermine white. So, what's he done, Mr. B? Whatever it is, I'll believe it. Strange guy. Very strange."

"I can't give you details, but attempted murder may be involved."

"Oh, dear."

"Any chance I could get a peek into his room, Tildy. I'm obviously not a cop but I'm acting on behalf of a very well known movie star and when all of this is over, I'll have him come by and thank you personally for your help."

She hesitates, then turns and takes a key down from a hook. "Room 12 first floor. This is the master key. Don't lose it and don't dawdle. If you get caught it's my job."

"Deal," I say with a smile and head off.

The door opens easily and I step inside. The room is clean and neat. Housekeeping at the Lodge is top notch. I don't know what I expect to find but I feel I'd be remiss if I didn't take a look. The license plate cinches it. There is no doubt that Cummings is my guy. Whether he actually tried to kill Marian Wagner or just frighten her, I don't know. I do know with some certainty that I am dealing with a certifiable weirdo. It's just possible I may stumble upon something concrete in the room that will tie him to the attempt, maybe not courtroom concrete but enough to persuade him to buy a return ticket to Heathrow on the next available plane.

The problem with a hotel room is there are only so many places to secrete something. Drawers, the closet, under the mattress. After that, where? How about an interior compartment in a suitcase? I look. Jackpot. Not very imaginative and, to be honest, the contents were not actually hidden. Just a couple of letters postmarked Belfast, Northern Ireland, from a woman named Marigold Toms and what appears to be a statement of royalties from a publishing company. From the looks of the minuscule amount that summed up his account's activity, its been quite a while since Cummings was a widely read author.

I skim Marigold's letters. She is in high dudgeon. Apparently Cummings had been living with (read: sponging off of) Marigold's mother Prunella for the past couple of years. Nuptials had been discussed but never acted upon even though the two lovebirds had exchanged wills. Then several months ago, Prunella was diagnosed with a virulent strain of cancer. Prunella would need personal care and lots of it which is when Horatio fortuitously discovered he was needed in the United States to write a screenplay. Forging Prunella's signature he cleaned out half her bank account, put her into a local hospice and left for the States, vowing to return a solvent man with a motion picture career ahead of him. Six weeks ago Prunella suffered a debilitating stroke, barely surviving. Horatio sent flowers with the card 'Much loved, much missed' but not loved or missed enough to return to Belfast.

At that moment there is a sharp knock on the door. I freeze, holding my breath. Silence. I don't like it. Horatio would have his key and Tildy would have called out my name. No, this is someone else.

"Cummings!" A sharp voice. Male. Another rap on the door, this one louder. He jiggles the doorknob. I look around, spot the sliding doors that lead to a patio that looks out toward the swimming pool. Quickly I replace the letters in their compartment and toss the suitcase back in the closet. I move swiftly to the glass door, slide it open and duck out. The pool area is deserted except for a waiter carrying a tray of drinks to a room at the far side of the Lodge. Like a good hotel employee he pretends not to notice me. I return the favor and when he is out of sight I jog quickly to the front office to return Tildy's key. I spend a moment or two flirting as I crane my head for a good look down the first floor corridor. Empty. Whoever it was, he's gone.

"The fella who just went down the corridor a minute or two ago, he say what he wanted?"

"What fella was that?" Tildy asks.

"He was pounding on the door to 12. He must have come through here."

She shakes her head.

"Probably entered through the rear door on the other side of the pool. It's supposed to be alarmed. It isn't."

I make a mental note never to check in here unless in the company of my trusty .25 caliber Beretta automatic. Meanwhile Tildy and I swear a binding oath that neither of us will mention to Cummings my visit to his room. On that note, I leave the cramped little office and head for my car.

I'm still a good twenty yards away when I spot it. My front left tire, as flat as a day old glass of cheap champagne. Upon inspection I find no nail, no tear in the sidewall and I am mystified. But not for long. A piece off paper is tucked under my windshield wiper. I remove it and scan the message which is short and to the point. 'Mind Your Own Business'. The man who was pounding on Cummings' door? I suspect so. I look carefully in every direction. Ideally I would spot a man jumping up and down and pointing to himself but I don't get that lucky. In fact I am very unlucky because whoever did this now knows me and my car and what we both look like.

I am hit-and-miss at hiding my concerns and my innermost feelings from my adorable wife, Bunny. I succeed about ten percent of the time. The other ninety percent I deal with the Inquisition. Yvette is at a neighbors down the street watching television with her very best friend Corky Bledsoe and Bunny and I are at the dinner table savoring pork chops and apple sauce when I look over at her. She is smiling like a Cheshire cat that has just spied a cheese-eating rat. I know that look well.

"Okay, what's going on?" she asks.

"What do you mean?"

"You're up to something you don't want me to know about."

"Nonsense."

"Don't 'nonsense' me, Joe Bernardi. The furtive looks, mind

elsewhere, monosyllabic sentences, unexplained phone calls. Oh, yes, Joe. I pick up, they hang up. I know you too well to think there's another woman but I wouldn't be surprised to learn you are neck deep in some funny business that is none of your concern."

"It is."

"It is what?"

"It is of my concern. Ever hear of someone named Wanda Periwinkle?"

"Oh, my God," she gasps, eyes widening.

"What?"

"I grew up with her books starting in fourth grade. Sultry looks, passionate kisses, heaving bosoms. Hot stuff for a pre-teen. I just loved her."

"Him."

"What him?"

"Wanda is a him named Horatio Cummings, craggy and misanthropic and very likely a serial stalker."

"You're kidding."

"I wish I was. There's every chance he tried to kill or injure Bob Wagner's wife which has caused Bob to be frightened enough for her safety to hesitate about committing to Sam August and if he doesn't do it, the picture will probably not get made so, yes, this guy is my concern."

"I can't believe it," she says.

"Believe it. We've got a witness," I reply.

"No, I mean I can't believe you're seriously thinking of Robert Wagner to play Sam August."

"That's because I know things you don't. He is a lot more than a no-talent dime-a-dozen juvenile."

"I'll take your word for it," she sighs, then shakes her head in bewilderment. "Wanda Periwinkle a guy, Robert Wagner an actor. Who knew?"

I'm up early the next morning and find Bunny munching reluctantly on one hardboiled egg, one glass of V8, three stalks of celery and a hot cup of tea, all intended to help her keep her girlish figure. If she doesn't watch out, vanity is going to transform her into Olive Oyl. She reminds me for the tenth time in the past two days that she and Yvette will not be home tonight, having been invited across town to a twelve girl slumber party and Bunny volunteering to be a chaperone. A kiss goodbye and then I am out the door heading toward Parker Center, formerly known as the Police Administration Building, and renamed a few days ago in honor of police chief William H. Parker. He suffered a fatal heart attack in early July and was much respected by the force and citizenry alike. The new guy has big shoes to fill. My good friend Lt. Aaron Kleinschmidt heads the homicide bureau and oversees all of the city's many divisions and when he sees me walk in the door, he knows that trouble is sitting on my shoulder.

"Unless this involves the murder of the Mayor, Joe, I haven't got time," he says looking up from the stack of paperwork strewn across his desk.

"No murder, Aaron. Not today," I say and tell him all about the attempt on Marian Wagner.

"And what has all this got to do with me?" he asks when I finally wind down.

"Attempted murder, Aaron," I say in annoyance. Aaron isn't usually this dense.

"No, Joe, until proved otherwise it's a traffic beef and you don't even know for sure that this guy Cummings was the driver—"

"I've got the plate number—"

"You've got a partial plate number—"

"Damned right I do. The car, the partial and I am here, Aaron, to see if you guys have anything on him or maybe we have to wait until it turns into an actual homicide before you or any of your toadies bothers to dig into it."

"Don't be petulant, Joe. I hate it when you get petulant."

"All I know is, if something does happen, Lou Cioffi is going to be all over this like paint on a picket fence."

"You're threatening me with the *L.A. Times?*" Aaron growls with a glare that would freeze a bonfire.

"No threat, Aaron. Lou doesn't need me to smell out a story, especially when a celebrity or his wife is involved. In fact he's already started sniffing around. I'm here only to get a little help, maybe a little background information but if you're too busy, I understand." I get to my feet. "Sorry I bothered you," I hiss as I head for the door.

"All right, all right," Aaron says, "I'll see if we have anything, but I'm telling you now, Joe, I'm not going to look after this guy on an 'if' and a 'maybe' or because he writes shitty books."

"Fair enough," I say. "I'll call you later."

Aaron forces a smile.

"No, Joe, I'll call you."

I get out while the getting's good.

I decide I need to check in with Wagner again, to show the flag, to persuade him I am working hard on his behalf to solve his problem. A call to the unit manager, Chuck Hansen, lets me know they are shooting at the Beverly House in Beverly Hills which is doubling for Lauren Bacall's lavish estate in the film. And yes, Robert Wagner is on call.

I hotfoot it over there. Jim Brown, the assistant director, has been told I'm coming. Nineteen years in the business and a Bentley for wheels opens a lot of doors in Hollywood in addition to the fact that I helped Chuck get a job at Warner's when he was first starting out. What goes around comes around, I think as I turn into the driveway at 1011 N. Beverly Drive and head for the main house which is a considerable distance in from civilization. I spot the transportation area and park and am climbing out of the car when I spot Paul Newman emerging from his motor home. He sees me and waves as he approaches.

"Hey, Joe, good to see you," Newman says smiling.

"Same here, Paul."

"I heard you were on the lot schmoozing with R.J. "

"You heard right."

"Word's also around that you're looking at him for your picture. I'm just a dumb actor but I'd grab him before somebody else does."

"You're far from dumb, old buddy, and your imprimatur means a lot."

"Nice of you to say so," he replies, "but Joanne seconds the motion. They did a picture together last year and she says Bob is the real deal."

"'A Kiss Before Dying'," I say.

"That's the one," Newman looks around, taking a deep breath of air. "You like this nice very warm air? Remind you of anything?"

"Yeah. Clinton, Louisiana, but without the smell of roadkill," I say.

He laughs. In '57 I spent a week with Newman and Joanne Woodward and the rest of the cast of 'The Long Hot Summer' putting together promotional material for the picture's release the following year. Judging by the box office we did a lousy job of it even though the picture got terrific reviews. Newman even got a Best Actor award at Cannes for his performance but bottom line, the business cares more about bucks than bravos. An artistic achievement but little else.

He and I start walking toward the imposing main house.

"You should have gotten here earlier," Newman says. "You missed all the excitement."

"Oh?"

"This cute little English bimbo, all curves and no straightaways, Mickey Rooney short, bleached blond with a cockney twist you could cut with a knife got past security and was trying to get to R.J. Security called the Beverly Hills cops and bounced her out of here and even when she was getting stuffed in the back of the squad car she was babbling undying love or something, not sure what."

"R.J. didn't know her?"

"Said he never saw her before. These creeps come with the territory, we both know that, and this one was a real whack job."

"Because?"

"Don't know, Joe. I just got the feeling she wasn't all there. Screwy, you know, and my guess is, none too bright. Odd though. R.J.'s been around these yo-yos all his life but with this one, I don't know, he seemed more shaken up than he should have."

"Is that right?"

"Yeah, that's right." We pause at the wide open front door, standing aside as the decorators and prop people moved in and out preparing for the next setup. Newman looks at me curiously. "Don't suppose you know anything about this guy Boxer that suddenly appeared out of nowhere?"

"Boxer? No. Should I?"

"Just seems strange. Joanne says Bob has had the same stand-in for years, an old school chum from Santa Monica High. Suddenly he's gone and Boxer's on the scene. Not a very friendly guy, by the way. Tight-lipped, doesn't say much."

"Like I said, don't know him."

"Okay, but I'm just saying, Joe, Bob's been kinda uptight lately and this thing with the cockney babe didn't help much."

"Thanks for the heads up," I say.

"Listen, Joe, tonight. What are your dinner plans?"

"Don't exactly have any," I say. "Bunny is chaperoning a pajama party to which my daughter has been invited. Why? Wanna break bread? It'll be nice to see Joanne again."

"Not here" he says. "Back home tending to the rose bushes and other homemaker duties. She's flying in this weekend."

"So, two guys on the town?"

"Why not? How about Scandia's. Eight o'clock," Newman suggests.

"Perfect," I say.

I go inside while Newman heads for the parking lot and his celebrated Maserati. It's no secret Paul's a sports car nut and is not so secretly developing a script with Howard Rodman about Grand Prix racing.

I find Wagner sitting close by the craft services table, coffee mug in hand, staring pensively at his shoes. He sees me coming and starts to get up. I wave him back down and pull up a nearby folding chair.

"I hear you had some excitement here this morning," I say.

"My adoring public. They come with the territory."

"I don't suppose you got a name."

"Name? No, why should I?" He hesitates and gives me a hard look. "Why should I, Joe? What have you found out?"

"Not much," I reply and then lay out my clandestine adventure at the Sportsman's Lodge.

Wagner shakes his head, puzzled.

"This flower, this Marigold, what's she got to do with me?"

"I don't know, Bob. Maybe nothing. Maybe I'm jumping to an erroneous conclusion but I don't think so."

"Sorry, but I never heard of her," Wagner replies. "Joe, look, I appreciate you are trying to help but you shouldn't get involved. Cosmo's on top of things,"

"Cosmo's a pretty good p.i. but he didn't discover the Sportsman's Lodge and besides that, I have a vested interest in helping you clear up this matter."

Wagner laughs. "I've heard you're a bulldog, Joe. You just proved it. Look, my ass is yours, okay. When this is done with, I'll sign on the dotted line for the film just as long as I have your word you'll be involved."

"I will be."

"Then fair enough. Now do me a favor and butt out. Cosmo and his guys will get this taken care of but I don't want you putting yourself at risk. Please, give me your word you'll stay clear until this situation is resolved. Then we'll make a picture together."

"You've got it," I say, "and my wife will be so pleased."

Wagner smiles.

"Smart wife you've got there," he says.

CHAPTER FIVE

Scandia's is an experience and if you have never been there, you would swear you were in a banquet hall of one of those Technicolor Robert Taylor medieval spectaculars. High ceilings, heraldic shields everywhere, the works except for a fatted pig roasting on a spit in the middle of the room. Everything apparently veddy veddy olde English except it's totally Scandinavian. Olde England the way the Vikings would have had it and probably did.

I spot Paul sitting at a small table in the rear and he's already working on his first beer. That's one of the things he and I have in common, beer, and we could do a lot worse than Tuborg, a house specialty. He greets me with a smile, then signals to our waiter, holding up his bottle and pointing at me. The waiter nods in comprehension and a couple of minutes later when he serves my beer, we order. Veal Oskar for me, poached salmon for Paul and gravlax for two to start. We chat amiably for a few minutes about the business, mutual friends and our families. I sense, however, that Paul is treading water. He has a topic he wants to get to so I lend him a hand.

"Obviously this lovely idea of yours entails more than idle chit chat so whenever you're ready, get to it."

He laughs.

"That's what I like about you, Joe. No wasted motion."

"Life's too short, Paul," I say.

"Amen to that," he replies. "Tell me about your latest book. The one in your typewriter."

"Haven't got one," I say.

"I was hoping you'd say that because I want to hire you, Joe. Thirty days at the outside and I will pay you handsomely."

"You need a script?" I ask.

"No, I need the old Joe Bernardi. The one I knew on the set of 'Long Hot Summer.'

"Sorry, my friend, I am out of that business and have been for quite a while."

"Not the way I heard it. You make exceptions. Got that straight from Bertha."

"Bertha talks too much. Anyway what the hell do you need a press agent for? You're a superstar."

"I'm a target for a handful of brain dead columnists and reporters out to make scoops where there are none. Sad about Newman suddenly reduced to starring in a run of the mill private eye movie. What's with this swelled-head Paul Newman changing Lew Archer to Lew Harper? More like a superstitious idiot just because his last two hit flicks started with the letter H. What's going on between Paul Newman and wife Joanne Woodward behind closed doors. Is trouble brewing between America's dream couple? How come Joanne's out and Janet Leigh is in as his lady love in his new flick for Warner Brothers. By the way, Joe, this is the same asshole who wrote a column wondering why no other leading ladies wanted to play opposite Newman, intimating Joanne had me on a short leash."

I shake my head, smiling.

"Paul, you can't let a few brain dead writers bother you. The woods are full of them, not just in the sticks but New York and Boston as well. The truth is, America loves you and Joanne and always will. Pay no attention."

"Easy for you to say, you don't have to read this junk."

"I read it all the time and I ignore it."

"I'm willing to pay you a great deal of money to put a stop to it."

"I couldn't even if I wanted to. These people have one ambition, to draw attention to themselves and they don't last long. The people who count know who and what you are, Paul."

"Yeah. Three time loser."

So that's it, I think. Three times up for a Best Actor Oscar and three times he's come up empty.

"I can't win an Oscar for you either, Paul. All you can do is pick the right material, give a great performance and then pray that the Gods are with you. Luck and timing are a huge part of who wins in any given year and we both know it. You are going to win one of these years and your press agent is going to have nothing to do with it."

"But—"

"But nothing," I say as our waiter approaches with our dinners. "Now shut up and eat your dinner."

He stares at me in momentary disbelief and then starts to laugh and then I laugh along with him.

"Yeah," he says, "but what about the guy who says I've been wearing contact lenses all my life just so my eyes can be bluer than Frank Sinatras?"

Now I laugh even harder as does he and then we are digging into our gravlax with abandon.

It's the next morning when I stumble out of bed. Bunny's still sleeping off a tough night with a dozen pajama clad pre-teens whose chief distractions seem to be destroying perfectly good pillows in warfare or mooning over Ricky Nelson or Bobby Darin or whoever's on the latest cover of Teenybopper Idols. I'm brushing my teeth and mentally recapping my conversation with Bob Wagner the previous afternoon.

I'm not exactly a liar but in the interest of expediency there are times I believe in telling people things I know they want to hear which is why I assured R.J. Wagner that I was going to butt out of his dilemma. I didn't mean a word of it. He needs tranquility in his life and I need him for my movie.

I grab a quick breakfast, then retire to my office and after some brief phone tag, I reach Horatio Cummings and invite him to meet me at twelve-thirty for lunch at Tom Bergin's Horseshoe Tavern, an enclave of the auld sod located near the Farmers Market. I'm just finishing up when Bunny appears in the doorway of my office. I wave her in as I am hanging up.

"Not interrupting?" she asks hopefully.

"Of course not," I say. "Come on in."

She comes in hesitantly.

"What's up?"I ask, knowing that something is.

"This Cummings—Wanda Periwinkle—you say he was a stalker?"

"Was and still is," I say.

"In one of her books—his books—the girl whose name was Mary—that's the name of the book, 'For the Love of Mary'—she was being stalked by this guy named Curtis all around the streets of Paris. She had a lover but Curtis didn't care. He was obsessed to the point where if he couldn't have her, nobody could. He makes her life a living hell and then there's a confrontation and an accident and Curtis thinks he's killed her. He didn't but he thinks he did and in agony he throws himself off the Eiffel Tower. She recovers and she and her lover live happily ever after."

"Sounds familiar," I say.

"I thought so, too," Bunny agrees.

"Too bad the Eiffel Tower is so far away."

"My thoughts exactly. You might want to share that with Cosmo."

"I will. Definitely."

"And let HIM follow through," she says firmly, casting an evil eye at me.

"You bet," I mumble.

"Who was that on the phone?" she asks.

I think fast.

"Jack Warner. We're having lunch. Something's going on with the studio. He wants to talk about it."

"You're not going back."

"Of course not."

"You heard the doctors. No stress. No excitement."

"It's lunch, Bunny. Just lunch."

"If you say so."

"I say so."

Bunny's been a nervous wreck ever since my mild heart attack late last year. If she had her way I'd be wrapped in a cocoon and locked in my room. If she were to learn I'm meeting with Cummings, she would freak out and so I don't tell her. In fact there are a lot of things I don't tell her these days and I hate myself for it but I will not be treated like a cripple.

I leave the house early in order to stop by Ben Tyler's book store, an emporium nearly as well stocked as the Library of Congress. When I tell Ben what I am looking for, he asks for a moment, disappears into the stacks and returns after a couple of minutes with a slim volume in hand. He grins. I grin back. Ben never fails me even when I ask the impossible.

On to the tavern which is unique and a real favorite of mine. The bar is well-stocked, the food is excellent and the ambience wavers between raucous and rowdy. I suppose I would be wise to back off and let others sort out Wagner's basket of snakes but there is something in my genes that forces me to plunge in whenever I am the least bit involved. Besides there's that British troublemaker who crashed the set demanding to see Wagner. With all that is going on with Horatio and the hit and run, I do not regard her appearance as coincidental. Hence, fool that I am, I will persevere until I get to the bottom of things.

I arrive first and grab a spot at the end of the bar. I order a Guinness, eschewing my usual Coors. The jukebox is playing "Galway Bay" and a half-dozen old timers who can't sing a lick are attempting to join in. Although letter perfect on the lyrics they spend a lot of time trying to find the right key and fail miserably.

He walks in the door at twelve-twenty-five and spots me immediately, smiling in the process. I wave to Paddy Grogan, the owner/ greeter/bouncer, and he catches on, leading Horatio to the bar and then, grabbing my Guinness, he takes us to our booth in the corner of the dining room. This is a prime location for favored clientele like me away from the clatter of cutlery and the babble of brogues, real and not so real, where Horatio and I can converse in relative peace. Horatio orders a double scotch, neat, and then settles back regarding me with what appears to be amused curiosity.

"Serendipity," he says reaching in his jacket pocket and taking out a briar pipe which he lights from a pack of matches lying next to an ashtray.

"Oh?" I say having no idea where this enigmatic remark is leading.

"As I said to you earlier, Mr. Bernardi, here I am a stranger in a strange land, trying valiantly to learn the secrets of writing a successful movie script from my first and most successful novel, 'The Enchanted Palazzo'. And then suddenly I am accidentally discovered by one of the industry's brightest up and coming screenwriters. Serendipity."

"I suppose," I say sipping my brew.

"And so here I am wondering how I can cajole you into offering a few tidbits on the art."

"Ah, you're here for a tutorial."

"Perhaps so and I might even pursue it as soon as I can figure out what you are doing here."

"Dining with a fellow scrivener, I believe."

"Yes, and I would be ready to believe that if I hadn't been tipped off otherwise by Rosalie the receptionist, who let it slip that a man matching your description had come to the production office hoping to learn of my whereabouts. Now I ask you, Mr. Bernardi, where is the serendipity in that?"

His scotch arrives and he downs half of it in one swallow, never losing his smug smile.

"None," I say, "but accidentally bumping into you makes for a much better story."

"For whom?"

"I lied, Mr. Cummings. I was never a fan of poetry. Mostly I am bewildered by it. It was my wife who studied poetry at college, dabbled unsuccessfully but still retains great admiration for many who were rejected by their peers but whose work endures. Like yours, Mr. Cummings."

Cummings laughs.

"Endures? What a quaint way of describing abject failure."

I reach in my jacket pocket and take out the slim volume I purchased from Ben Tyler. I slide it across the table.

"I know Bunny will be thrilled if you would sign this for her," I say.

He picks it up, studies it shaking his head in disbelief.

"'Reflections on a Cotswold Bridge'," he says. "I can't believe the damned thing is still in print." He smiles up at me. "It has always been my most treasured failure. Do you have a pen?"

I reach in my pocket and hand him one.

"Her name is Bunny," I say.

"Lovely," he replies, scrawling an inscription on the title page.

"I would have brought one for Marian as well but this was the only one left in stock."

"Marian?"

"A good friend. She told us she knew you some years ago. Overseas. Paris or London."

His hand freezes over the book for a fraction of a second before he continues writing. Then he shakes his head. "I've lived in London for most of my life, Mr. Bernardi, but I really don't remember an American woman named Marian."

"Funny, I didn't say she was American," I smile, "though she is. At the time she was married to the film director, Stanley Donen."

Cummings looks up, sliding the book back toward me.

"Can't say that I recall her," he says.

"Of course you do. You stalked her all over London professing undying love while Donen was putting Bergman and Grant through their paces at rain-drenched locations. Incidentally you don't seem to have given it up. The stalking, I mean."

His wary look has morphed into an icy glare.

"What is it you want from me, Mr. Bernardi?"

"For starters you might tell me who the woman was who stormed onto the Warners set this morning, demanding to see Robert Wagner."

"Don't know what you're talking about," he says.

"Voluptuous bleached blond, very short, with a cockney accent straight out of Charles Dickens."

His face has frozen, betraying nothing. I remind myself not to play cards with the man. Slowly he shakes his head.

"Sorry, you've been dealt some false information," Cummings says. "Earlier you said, for starters. Please continue."

"I want you to stay away from Bob and Marian Wagner. Far away, Mr. Cummings. I am very close to highly placed officers in the Los Angeles Police Department. Either I make your life here in Los Angeles a living hell or I see you off on a flight back to London with a decent bottle of Dom Perignon as a going away present."

"Like that," he says quietly.

"Like that," I say even more quietly.

"A pity you don't know the whole story, Mr. Bernardi,"

Cummings says. "Whole? Hell, man, you don't even know half of it and you certainly don't know the best half."

"Suppose you tell me."

"Don't know why I should but yes, I'll humor you. Marian Donen did hold a certain fascination for me back then, mainly because she seemed to be the embodiment of the strong female characters I was used to creating. I wanted to get to know her better so that I could make her, using a fictional name, of course, as the centerpiece of the new novel I was contemplating. She mistook my intentions, things got out of hand and suddenly I found myself depicted as a loathsome predator in the tabloids. Columnists vilified me, cartoonists mocked me and I became a laughing stock. Sales of my books fell off and my publisher dropped me. It took me two years to find another one. Was I angry? Yes. Bitter? Perhaps. Vindictive? No. I wanted to be left alone to lick my wounds and I did."

"So you bear Marian Wagner no ill will."

"Of course not."

"And you haven't been driving past her house, observing her from afar."

"I have not."

"And a few days ago, you didn't try to run her down in the middle of an intersection."

"That is an insane accusation!" he says loudly.

I look around uncomfortably. People are starting to stare.

"If you did, Mr. Cummings, I intend to prove it," I say.

He hesitates, then slides out of the booth and stands, hovering over me. He is in a rage and does nothing to disguise it.

"Don't you dare to threaten me, Bernardi, you third rate hack of a writer!"

I continue to glance around as quiet descends and eyes from all corners of the room focus on us.

"You are making a scene."

"And you, sir, are a son of a bitch."

"Keep your voice down," I say sharply.

"Bloody hell I will!" Cummings says. "Keep away from me, Bernardi, and that goes for your friend Wagner as well. I mean it. I make a very dangerous adversary."

With that he turns on his heel and strides toward the front entrance, ignoring the gazes of the shocked and curious who look from him to me and back again. I watch him leave. So much for getting to the bottom of things.

I get up and walk to the front desk where I drop a Jackson on the counter.

"Sorry, Paddy," I say.

"You keep sordid company, Mr. Bernardi," he replies, palming the twenty. "If I'd known he was an Englishman, I never would have let him in the door."

"Won't happen again," I grin and go out, ruing my clumsiness. Was it Twain who said that no good deed goes unpunished? Right now I just want to go home, and curl up on the sofa leaving the woes of Robert Wagner for others to sort out.

Wednesday morning. I sleep late if you can call 9:13 late. Usually I'm up and about by eight o'clock but not today. I just roll over and ignore the sun streaming in the bedroom window. Then the phone rings. Grumbling, I reach for it. Still grumbling, I answer.

"This better be good," I say.

"Mr. Bernardi?"

"Who's this?"

"Paddy Grogan. Sounds like I woke you up."

"You'd make a good detective, Paddy. What's up?"

"Look, I didn't rat you out, not really."

"Good to hear. Rat me out how?"

"About the Englishman."

"What about him?"

"He's dead."

"Dead?"

"Dead. Then the cops haven't contacted you yet."

"No. What do you mean, dead? How did he die?"

"He was mugged. At least I think that's it. They found a pack of matches from the restaurant in his shirt pocket. That's why they showed up at my door just before seven o'clock."

The intercom on my nightstand crackles.

"Sir, are you awake?" Bridget's voice.

"I'm on the phone, Bridget," I tell her, pressing the com button.

"There's two coppers at the door wantin' to see you, sir," she says. "Shall I shoo them away?"

I hesitate. This can be nothing but bad news.

"Tell 'em I'll be right down." Then, into the phone. "Paddy, thanks for the tipoff. I'll call you later."

The guy in the living room screams 'cop' from the cheap suit and black brogues to the bulge under his left arm pit. He's pudgy and white haired and wearing a face that's seen too many dead bodies and doesn't want to see any more. He also sports that 'don't fuck with me' look that a lot of cops project to make sure guys like me know who's in charge. He's staring at our wedding photo which is framed and propped up on the mantlepiece. He turns toward me when I clear my throat and manages a semi-sincere smile.

"Your wife's a real looker," he says just for something to say.

"Thanks. I was told there were two of you," I say.

"My partner's using the facility," he says, walking toward me as he displays his badge. "Hugo Schapp, Detective Two out of Van Nuys. I have a few questions."

"Sure."

By now he's right on top of me, invading my personal space. I notice his eyes are slightly bloodshot and his breath smells like Sen-Sen.

"Are you acquainted with a Mr. Horatio Cummings, Mr. Bernardi?"

"I am." I try to back away. He steps even closer.

"And when was the last time you saw him?"

"Alive, you mean?"

His eyes narrow suspiciously.

"That's right. Alive," he says. He casually unbuttons his jacket so I can get a good look at his service revolver. This guy's deeply into intimidation.

"I was with him yesterday for lunch at the Horseshoe," I say, "but you already know that or you wouldn't be here."

Another hard look.

"Are you trying to get smart with me?" he asks.

"No, just looking for a little breathing room," I say, trying to move away from him. Just then I look toward the foyer. Detective Pete Rodriguez appears, wringing his hands dry. An old friend, we've known each other for years. He throws me a smile.

"How's it going, Joe?" he asks.

"Not sure, Pete. Ask me in a few minutes. Your partner's been grilling me up close and personal. Either that or he's been trying to seduce me."

"Wise guy," Schapp says to Pete with a scowl.

"Always has been," Pete says. "How about some coffee, Joe?"

"Sure, let's go in the kitchen."

A couple of minutes later we're seated at the kitchen table with hot mugs of coffee in front of us, courtesy of Bridget, who has now scooted off to let us talk in private.

"So, what happened?" I ask. Pete, always pleasant and obliging, tells me.

"He was found by sanitation workers around six in the morning in the alley behind the Sportsman's Lodge. Two .45 slugs, one on the gut and another in the heart. It was supposed to look like a mugging but even Joe Friday could have smelled this one out. His wallet was empty, lying by his side, but the killer neglected to take his diamond pinkie ring and his Piaget wrist watch worth at least a grand, maybe more. Blood evidence indicates he was killed elsewhere and dumped."

"Time of death?" I ask.

"Between two and four in the wee hours of the morning," Rodriguez says. "So what do you think?"

"Hard to grasp a motive, Pete," I say. "He told me he knew nobody here in L.A aside from the movie company he was hired by."

"And you," Hugo Schapp growls.

"I didn't really know him," I reply.

"Then why were you having lunch with him, Joe?" Pete asks quietly.

The can is now open and the worms are wriggling every which way. If I leave Wagner and his missus out of this I do so at my own peril. If I give them up, this suddenly becomes a very, very messy situation, especially with Lou Cioffi sniffing about for a scoop. Thinking quickly I do what I always do when put into this kind of bind. I invent a fairy tale.

"Cummings' nom de plume—"

"His what?" Hugo Schapp grunts dully.

"His alias. His pen name. He wrote women's romance novels under the name Wanda Periwinkle. He was in Los Angeles writing a screenplay from one of his books which Regal King Productions was going to turn into a cheapie programmer." Schapp still looks blank. "B movie. Bottom end of a double feature which they still show out in Idaho somewhere."

"And you are involved how?" Pete asks.

"Okay, so a friend tells me he's in town because this friend knows that Bunny loves the guy's books even though Bunny still thinks this guy is a babe named Wanda Periwinkle. I track Cummings down and reach out for this lunch date hoping I could get to know him, then cajole him into maybe coming to the house the next night for one of Bridget's fabulous meals and make myself the hero of the century to Bunny. And that's it. That's as sinister as it gets, Pete."

"Uh-huh," he mutters, oozing doubt and disbelief. "And this big brouhaha you had in front of several dozen witnesses?"

"He was anti-social, hated taking meals with fans."

"How does that square with him accusing you of threatening him, Joe?"

"I didn't threaten him, Pete, he threatened me."

" And who's this guy Wagner he was bellyaching about?"

"You mean Morris Wagner," I say.

"I don't know. Do I?"

"When we'd made our dinner plans, he asked me if I knew a reliable turf accountant—"

"You mean, bookie."

"That's right. Bookie," I say, paddling upstream as fast as I can and losing badly. I can tell from the way Pete's eyes are glazing over, this is not going well. "I gave him Morris' name and number and I guess they had some sort of disagreement for which Cummings held me responsible—"

"Okay, okay," Pete says. "I can take only so much of this, Joe. What is it you're trying to hide?"

I hesitate. There is no way in hell I can tell him about Bob Wagner and his wife who will be delighted to learn that their tormenter has been dispatched to the nether world. They are most assuredly innocent but it won't matter. The press will roast them daily with innuendo and half-truths.

"I can't tell you, Pete, but I can assure you it has nothing to do with the mugging death of your victim."

"Hey, bright boy," Schapp jumps in. "It wasn't no mugging. Wasn't you paying attention?"

I glare at him but before I can skewer him with a witty riposte, Pete intervenes. "Hugo, wait outside. I need to speak to Mr. Bernardi privately."

"Hey, partner—" he starts to say.

"I'm the sergeant, Hugo. You're not. Wait in the car."

Schapp starts to say something, then shaking his head, turns on his heel and heads in the direction of the front door. When he's out of earshot, Pete turns back to me.

"He's an old war horse, Joe. By the book and only by the book but he's retiring next month. Right now he's just crossing the days off his calendar."

"I understand."

"So now that it's just you and me, let's hear it. Off the record."

"None of this goes in your report."

"My ears only. At least for now, Joe. Let's have it."

So I tell him what I know and he listens intently. When I'm finished he shakes his head.

"Robert Wagner, huh? I'm going to have to check this out, Joe."

"I know but just you, Pete. Not your partner and nothing in writing."

"Can do unless and until I find the Wagners are involved. Then all bets are off."

I nod.

"Wouldn't have it any other way," I say already regretting what I have done and knowing also that I really had no choice.

"Look, Pete, I know I'm asking a lot but maybe you could back away for a day or two while I dig around. I might stumble across something that'll make your job easier."

"Funny you should ask, Joe," Pete says. "I'm taking a couple of personal days starting tomorrow. Me and the family are driving down to Chula Vista for my father-in-law's 65th birthday."

"I can do a lot in two days, Pete," I say.

"Don't," he says firmly.

"I can't just sit around—"

"I said don't, Joe. Aaron may humor you. I won't. Let me do my job." I hesitate, then nod. "I mean it, Joe. Don't muck things up."

"I hear you, Pete. Your case, you handle it."

Even as I say the words, I only half mean them. In three days leads freeze up and I wouldn't trust Hugo Schapp to find a pool cue in a billiard parlor.

CHAPTER SIX

I need to speak to Cosmo Stryker right away. When I call his office, I am surprised to learn that he is at his desk negotiating a security contract with some well known rock and roll idol. The Wagners are presumably being covered by minions. Cosmo can't be disturbed by phone so I warn his Gal Friday, Lola, that I'm on my way, then hop in the car and drive to Cosmo's digs on Little Santa Monica Boulevard. I park on the street across from his storefront headquarters and head for the entrance just as a somewhat familiar figure from the music world is emerging. I can't quite remember his name but he's one of those one-hit wonders who is fast sinking into oblivion and needs a bodyguard like I need shingles. Once again this confirms my belief that self-delusion is a disease shared by all the second-raters in show business.

Cosmo is not happy that I have brought the police into the Wagner situation. He cares not a whit that I had no choice or that, for the moment, it's on a confidential basis. He's the one who will have to answer to R.J., not me. On the other hand he is delighted that I have apparently identified the man who tried to run down Marian Wagner and even happier to learn that he is dead. His smile fades as he stares up at the ceiling and frowns. He's troubled by something.

"What's gnawing at you, Cosmo?" I ask.

"I'd feel better if we had a one hundred per cent identification on this guy but I don't fancy showing a morgue mug shot to an eleven-year-old kid."

"I know where to find a photo of Cummings in livelier days if you really think it's necessary."

"I do, just to be on the safe side."

"I'll do what I can," I say. "You do realize, Cosmo, that Cummings' death is not necessarily good news for the Wagners."

"I'm way ahead of you, Joe. I can only hope the two of them have solid alibis for the time of the bastard's death."

I change the subject by asking him what he knows, if anything, about the woman who invaded the movie location.

"Not a thing and the Beverly Hills cops aren't talking, at least not to me. Last year one of my guys got caught sitting in a backyard tree taking photos inside the master bedroom of one of filmdom's biggest leading ladies, publicly a Nice Nellie but privately a sucker for anything in pants. And when I say sucker, I mean sucker."

"The cops didn't mention the name Marigold Toms?" I ask.

"They mentioned only that I should get my ass out of Beverly Hills and stay out. Who is this Marigold anyway?"

"Not sure."

"Let me know when you find out," Cosmo says.

"Will do," I say. "Meanwhile I'll see what I can do about that photograph."

With a sigh, I hop in my car and motor back to King Regal Productions where I park in an empty space one down from a fire hydrant. I glance across the street and catch Pedro's eye. The old horse thief is going to have to do without my business, at least for today. I'm positive the hit-and-run driver was Cummings but there's a remote possibility it could be some other white haired bearded psycho. After a couple of minutes using the public convenience on the first floor, I walk through the door to discover Rosalie chatting with some guy whose back is to me. It's only when he turns toward me that I recognize Garrison King from that same photo on the wall. Rosalie introduces me and King breaks into an warm smile and shakes my hand effusively, then invites me into his private office. For a guy whose name screams Oxford don, his accent screams prison guard at Auschwitz.

"Gerhardt Koenig, Mr. Bernardi. That is my birth name," he says indicating the chair across from his desk. I sit as he continues. "I could not help noticing your reaction to my Germanic accent. The war still lingers in the minds of many and grudges continue to be held against me and my fellow Deutschlanders. Hence, my industry identity."

"Maybe you should work up a brogue or a Scottish burr to go with the name," I suggest.

"Beyond my powers. I am a first rate producer. I leave performing to others." He sits up in his chair, ramrod stiff. "Now, sir, you came earlier to these offices looking for Mr. Cummings so I must presume you know I am taking his first novel to the screen. It was and is a popular book. I think it will do well."

"Especially with the author of the book writing the screenplay."

"No, it will prosper despite Mr. Cummings involvement. He is a terrible writer. The screenplay was made part of the deal at his insistence and now I must find a way to work around his participation or my deal for the rights will be, how do you say it, Mr. Bernardi? Kablooey?"

"As good a word as any. So you have the rights as long as Cummings writes the script and if he doesn't, you don't have the rights. That about it?"

"In a word, *jawohl*. Now you must understand, Mr. Bernardi, 'The Enchanted Palazzo' is a terrible book, overwritten, cliched and maudlin and that is just for starters. However it happens to be a favorite of a popular but brain-dead up-and-coming young actress born of a well known Hollywood family who has agreed to play the lead at half her usual quote and I have this in writing. She has also agreed to forego her obnoxious pro-communist public appearances during the shooting of the film and for ninety days following it's general release."

"I can guess who this Marxist chick is. Why would she suppress her politics merely for the sake of a movie role?"

"Because," King says, "I am paying her a fortune to do so. Believe me her silence did not come cheap but in the end Mammon won out over self-indulgence. So you see, Mr. Bernardi, my hands are clasped around a multi-million dollar gold mine, a deal flawed only by the participation of the equally brain dead writer."

"In that case, Mr. King, I may be the bearer of good tidings," I say. "Horatio Cummings is dead and not just his brain."

He is startled and it looks genuine. Either I have surprised him or he is more of a performer than he lets on.

"Do not jest, sir. I am no longer a young man. My heart cannot deal with it", he says.

"He was killed last night a short distance from the Sportsman's Lodge. It was staged to look like a robbery. It wasn't. The police are all over it."

King's face morphs from disbelief into mock despair.

"Poor Horatio. Such an unhappy man. Now he is at peace although I am not. I am in dire need of a writer."

"Of course, now that there is no hindrance to your claim on the material," I remind him.

"Exactly so, Mr. Bernardi."

"I'm digging around into the circumstances of his death, Mr. King, and you may be able to help me."

"I can't possibly see how," King says. "I was in a late night poker game with several friends well into the wee hours of the morning. It is a regular affair, held every Wednesday evening at my condo. I believe we broke up shortly past two a.m. I can supply names of the other players if needs be."

Lucky me. I didn't ask him for an alibi but he was only too happy to provide everything but the train schedule to Cucamonga. Iron clad. Unbreakable, And seven people to boot. Wow!

"What do you know about a woman named Marigold Toms?"

"Nothing," he says.

"Never met her?"

"No. Should I have?"

"I'm not sure."

"You suspect she might be involved in Mr. Cummings death."

"It's possible," I say.

"Well, I know nothing about either the woman or the murder," King says and then his eyes narrow and his lips curl into a faint smile. "I understand you are a screenwriter, Mr. Bernardi."

"On occasion," I reply.

"I may have work for you."

"Not 'The Enchanted Palazzo'. Thanks anyway."

"But I have not told you the excellent writing fee I am prepared to pay nor the name of the actress in question."

Having not done so, now he does. The pay is barely adequate. It's the actress who has me intrigued. I had already guessed at her name but,indeed, she is the attractive ingenue in a famed Hollywood family of actors, her father being a major leading man for nearly thirty years though not yet an Oscar winner. She has been working steadily for the past five or six years and has the looks and the talent so why would she want to get involved in this loser of a picture? And then I remember the 'brain dead' part which brings back images of her and a thousand like her storming City Hall with protest signs reading 'Save the Whales' when it was painfully obvious in her post-protest interviews that she had no idea what she wanted to save them for.

"Actually, Mr. King, the reason I am here is not to deliver the news of Mr. Cummings demise but to borrow a photo of the man."

"For what purpose?"

"It also has to do with the investigation into his death. I was thinking of the photo on your anteroom wall. I could return it to you tomorrow."

He smiles and reaches into a desk drawer.

"I can do better than that, Mr. Bernardi," he says, handing me an 8x10 glossy. "Horatio insisted I have these made up in advance of a major publicity campaign. I found it expedient to humor him."

Cummings' visage is serious but it's a good likeness.

"I presume I can keep this," I say.

"Of course. And as to the adaption of the novel—?"

"Let me sleep on it," I say. "I'll let you know tomorrow."

"Fair enough," King says, rising from his chair and extending his hand. We shake. I hate stringing him along but if something unexpected comes up, I want to retain access to him.

I walk out into the sunlight. My car is parked ticketless where I left it but now the space next to the fire hydrant is occupied by a late model cream-colored Cadillac El Dorado with the license plate 'THE KING'. A funny thing has happened however. The fire hydrant has disappeared. Why do I now think it was made of papier maché and is probably sitting in the trunk of the Cadillac. I slip behind the wheel of my beloved Bentley and pull out into traffic I pay scant attention to the black Ford Fairlane parked across the street and am oblivious to the fact that he has pulled a U-ey and is fifty yards back following my every move.

Cosmo is not in his office but I leave the photo with Lola. I tell her I can be reached at home after six o'clock and scrawl my number on the back of the glossy. Once again I head for my car, glancing at my wrist watch. It is nearly one o'clock. I missed breakfast and now I am in danger of missing lunch as well. It can't be helped. I have a stop to make and best to get it over with. Cosmo had no luck with the Beverly Hills cops but as far as I know they bear me no ill will. I suppose I am about to find out. I pull out into traffic. This time I notice the black Ford sedan sliding into the traffic behind me. I also notice a somewhat beat up green VW bug joining the parade. I know I've seen that car before but I can't remember where.

The Beverly Hills cops are housed at City Hall and are regarded by some as a tea and crumpets organization, not particularly effective and generally intimidated by the wealth and celebrity that surrounds them. In this they are sadly mistaken. The citizenry pay for the best and expect the best and most of the time they get it. The dregs of Los Angeles have learned the hard way to stay clear of this privileged enclave. I pull into the parking lot and exit my car. The Ford pulls in a few moments later and parks some distance away. No one exits the car. Not many people in Los Angeles drive plain stripped down black Fords with black wall tires and a whip antenna. Those that do usually carry a badge. I start inside glancing momentarily toward the street. The green Volkswagen has hesitated near the entrance to the parking lot but now as I peer at it, the driver pulls away. I'm not used to this attention and my curiosity has been piqued.

The desk sergeant is a matronly female with short cropped hair and beady eyes that exude suspicion. I tell her I need to speak to the detective who handled the movie location disruption the previous day. What for, she asks. My business, I reply. Her eyes get beadier. She points to a wooden bench and suggests that I sit down while she tries to locate the sergeant. I do as I'm told while she goes back to her paperwork. I believe she's using mental telepathy to contact the sergeant as she makes no move to pick up her phone. I decide to give her five minutes, no more, before I ask to see the chief, Clint Anderson, whom I can palm off as a close personal friend. An exaggeration. Several years ago he was the tech advisor on a Warner's cop drama for which I was beating the drum. Once or twice we shared burgers and fries at the lunch break.

Two minutes pass and then a beefy guy in slacks and an ill-fitting sports jacket saunters in, heading to the elevators. The desk sergeant waves him over and points to me. He looks. His expression is even beadier than hers. He nods to her and then heads in my direction.

"I'm Sergeant Hoffman. You are?" I give him my name. He nods. "How can I help you, Mr. Bernardi?"

"I'm curious about the woman who crashed the 'Harper' set yesterday morning. Miss Toms. I believe."

"And who told you that?"

"I have my sources."

"Good for you. Again, who gave you the woman's name?"

"I'm working unofficially with the investigative firm protecting Mr. Wagner and his family."

"You mean that dirtbag Cosmo Stryker."

"I'm not at liberty to say."

"Too bad," Hoffman shrugs. "You have a nice day now," he says as he turns and keeps moving toward the elevator. I call after him.

"In the event that something unfortunate happens to Mr. Wagner or a member of his family, I'll be back talking to Chief Anderson. Your name will be prominently mentioned, Sergeant. And oh, yes, I'll be accompanied by Lou Cioffi. Nothing Lou loves more than a juicy story about police stupidity." Every cop in the city knows who Lou is. They also know they don't want to see their names mentioned in his column.

"Now may I speak to her or not?" I ask.

Hoffman stops short, turns and waves me forward, regards me curiously.

"Bernardi?"

"That's right."

"Aaron Kleinschmidt's pal."

"We know each other."

"You're some kind of writer."

"That's right."

"He says you're a pain in the ass."

"He should know."

"And a wise guy."

"That, too."

He hesitates momentarily.

"Follow me," he says.

A couple of minutes later we're sitting at his desk in the squad room. He's poured himself a cup of coffee. I received no such hospitality.

"Kleinschmidt says you're not entirely stupid."

"Nice of him."

"You also stick your nose into police business where it doesn't belong—"

"Not if I can help it."

"—but once in a while you actually come up with something useful."

"Once in a while," I agree.

Hoffman reaches in his pocket, extracts a Chesterfield from a near empty pack and lights up. All the while he keeps his gaze fixed on me.

"The name on her passport is Marigold Toms. She flew into L.A. four days ago. She's registered at a fleabag motel near the airport. She claims to be an advertising executive but she carries no business cards and she's here on a 30 day visitor visa. She's been accompanied by a slightly younger man whose name may or may not be Dylan Pfieffer. She claims she wanted to talk to Wagner about a British television endorsement for something called Weetabix."

"And?"

"And she also claims to be a woman which, as far as I can tell, may be the only truthful statement she made to me. Now, your turn, Mr. Bernardi. What's your interest in this woman?"

"Can't say, Sergeant. I'm working in concert with Cosmo Stryker and there's a matter of client confidentiality."

"Bullshit."

"Do you know Pete Rodriguez? Homicide sergeant working out of the Valley?"

"I know him."

"Give him a call. He may be able to help you."

"Homicide?"

"It's a long story. Now may I speak to her?"

"No."

"No?"

"I kicked her loose yesterday afternoon."

"Why?" I ask in disbelief.

"Because I had nothing to hold her on."

"Trespass."

"Get real. Anyway I had no idea that she was public enemy number one."

I shake my head and ask him for the name of the motel Marigold is staying at near the airport. At first he is reluctant to give it to me but when I promise to share anything I learn he relents. We part on a reasonably good note.

I walk out into the parking lot. The green Volkswagen is missing but the black Ford is right where I left it and there is someone sitting behind the wheel. Okay, enough's enough. Time to find out what's going on. I walk past the Bentley and head straight for the Ford. He or she must have seen me coming because the engine fires up and the car lurches from its spot and heads in the opposite direction. I'm just close enough to get the plate number which I scrawl on the back of my left hand with my ballpoint pen. I'm pretty sure I know where this car has come from and who is driving it so my only real question is, why.

CHAPTER SEVEN

I suppose I should chase down Marigold Toms at the fleabag motel down by the airport. I could also drive to Van Nuys and corner Detective Second Class Hugo Schapp to find out why he is following me all over Hell's half acre because if there is one thing I am sure about, it's been Schapp behind the wheel of that damned unmarked black Ford. But the truth is, I am tired and irritable and for the moment, I've had quite enough of this tail chasing that's taken up most of the day and all of my good will. I want to see the smiling faces of my two best girls so I head for home. My watch reads a few minutes to five.

I turn onto Franklin Avenue and immediately spot him. The beat up VW bug is parked at curbside in front of my house and now I remember who owns the damned thing. As I go by, ready to turn into my driveway, Lou Cioffi throws me a smile and a wave. I smile back. I've just exited my car and already he is trudging up the driveway to greet me.

"You've been busy," he says.

"Never a dull day," I respond.

"A visit to Cosmo Stryker, then the Beverly Hills cops. What am I missing, Joe?"

"Not a thing, Lou."

"No shit. Tell me about the stiff they found this morning near the Sportsman's." He takes out a small pad and consults it. "Horatio Cummings. Have I got that right?"

"Don't know what you're talking about," I say and seeing the look in Lou's eyes regretting it immediately.

"I don't have much, Joe, but I've got enough and you're a lying son of a bitch."

Now I feel like crap because on many occasions Lou has compromised his journalistic ethics to help me and Pete and Aaron right wrongs.

"You're right. I am."

"Tell me," Lou says.

"I can't. First of all, facts are skimpy. Most what I've got is speculation. You'd be in litigation overnight. Secondly, just a whiff of this story in print and some very nice people are going to be badly hurt. I can't allow that, Lou. I'm sorry."

"And in the future?" he asks cautiously.

"That's different. Under the right circumstances I—that is, we— me and Pete Rodriguez and Cosmo Stryker—could hand you a dandy exclusive because so far nobody but you has come within sniffing distance of putting the two events together."

"An exclusive."

"Provided the situation is resolved and no innocent people get hurt."

"You mean Wagner."

I hesitate for a moment.

"I mean Wagner and his family." He nods thoughtfully. "I'm asking you to lay off, Lou. If there's a story, you get it. If there isn't I'll fill you in and count on you not to violate my trust. You know me well enough to know I wouldn't put it this way if it weren't critical."

"Okay, pal, I'll play along. Give me a buzz when you can give me something."

"You'll be my first and only call."

He nods, then throws me a little salute and starts back toward his car. I watch him drive away, relieved. If nothing else, Lou Cioffi is a man of his word. Any leakage won't be coming from him. I turn and head for the front door.

As soon as I walk in the door, I am confronted with my wife's face and it isn't smiling. She walks straight toward me, stops, hands on hips, and snarls, "What the hell have you been up to?"

"Excuse me," I say blankly.

"Why in hell was Lou Cioffi parked out in front of the house for the past thirty minutes?"

"He's working on a story——"

"I'm away from you for nineteen hours and twenty minutes and in my absence I learn you have been questioned by the police in regard to a corpse discovered in Studio City."

"Yes. Horatio Cummings."

"Well, I suppose I'm pleased that at least you know the man's name and that he isn't a complete stranger."

"Bunny——"

"My God, Joe, you have completely forgotten the heart attack you suffered less than a year ago and the advice given to you by both your doctors, to stay quiet, avoid unnecessary exertion, and involve yourself with criminal activity only on the pages that pour out of your typewriter."

"I'm fine——"

"You're not fine. You don't sleep well, your eating habits are deplorable, and your digestive processes are wildly unpredictable."

"Not really——"

"Do the police actually believe you killed this man Cummings——?

"Ridiculous——!"

"——because that's the impression this detective gave Bridget when he came back to question her around eleven thirty——"

"Now wait a minute—"

"—to verify your alibi that you were here in the house at the time the man was killed and a piss poor alibi it is since we both know and now the cops know that Bridget is somewhere between hard of hearing and stone deaf and some years ago probably slept through huge sections of World War Two." Tears start to drain from her eyes.

"And while we're at it, who the hell is Katherine Drexel?"'

"What?"

She reaches in her pocket and takes out a small sheet of note-pad paper. "Katherine Drexel. Texas. KKK. Two dead. Call after seven o'clock," she reads, then looks at me. "I found this in your blue blazer when it came back from the cleaners. I know you too well to be worried about another woman but what's this 'two dead' business and the Ku Klux Klan? Is this another murder you just can't keep your hands off of, Joe? Is Katherine one of your old schoolteachers or maybe a long lost aunt that came to you for help? Which is it, Joe? Tell me. I love a good story."

She sobs, losing control. I grab her by her arms and pull her toward me, planting a big wet one on her lips. She struggles for about a half a second and then melts and weeps softly in my arms.

"She's a nun, Bunny," I say softly, "actually a Saint, and she died years ago. It's a true story someone told me about. I was going to follow up on it but never got to it."

"I'm sorry," she whispers quietly, clinging to me. "I'm just so scared—"

"I know,I know, babe," I say, holding her close. "You're right. I kind of got dragged into this current mess. We're trying to get Bob Wagner for the picture and there are problems. Big problems."

"Tell me."

"It's a long story."

"Tell me anyway."

"Sure," I say, taking her by the arm and leading her into the kitchen where I grab a Nehi from the fridge and she pours a cup of coffee from the percolator. We sit down at the table and I tell her all about the Wagners and the sudden appearance of Horatio Cummings, presumptive stalker, now toes up at the county morgue.

"Walter Mirisch is right," I say. " We wanted Redford but the more I see of Wagner, the more I realize he's an excellent choice to play Sam August. And he says he will, as soon as this mess gets straightened out. The problem is, dealing with a possible stalker was one thing, dealing with a dead stalker whose death was staged to look like a robbery is something else again. Talk about a suspect list, the Wagners are right at the top of it."

"The police will sort it out, Joe," she says looking me squarely in the eyes. I squirm a little. Her message is clear. Stay out of it.

"I know, Bunny. I know. None of my business," I say, half meaning it.

"Joe, I'm not going to stop checking up on you. I love you too much to sit back and let you risk your well being on fools' errands."

"I understand," I say.

"I'm not sure you do," she says. "You may think you're Don Quixote, you're not, and I am not Dulcinea. You're a middle aged man who has his priorities all screwed up and I'm not going to put up with it, not any more."

"Okay," I say sheepishly. I think she believes me. I almost believe it myself.

Later, dinner is dominated by a bubbly Yvette who enchants us with juvenile gossip culled from the p.j. party. I smile a lot but I have no idea what she is talking about. Neither does Bunny but we play along. We make it all the way to dessert when I am called away from my dish of rocky road to take a call from my friend, Ray Giordano, Southern California's most notorious criminal defense attorney.

"Yo," I say into the phone.

"Yo yourself," Ray says. "What the hell have you been up to?"

"Is this a trip to the woodshed? I've already had one of those today and from someone a lot prettier than you are."

"Tell me about Horatio Cummings."

"He's dead."

"That I know. Cosmo Stryker has put me together with Robert Wagner, the actor, on the possibility that Wagner may need representation in Cummings' death."

"A wise move."

"So I learned when I asked around. I also learned that unofficially you are running a close second on the suspect list."

"Me? Horse manure," I say.

"You tracked him to the office where he was working and then accidentally ran into him at an open air cafe."

"I can explain—"

"You invited him to lunch at the Horseshoe where you got into a very public screaming match even before you'd ordered—"

"He screamed, I didn't—"

"And you have no legitimate alibi for the time he was murdered."

"I suppose—"

"You suppose? Look, Joe, I'm perfectly happy to get involved with Wagner but not if the cops are coming after you. I can't represent you both."

"I'll be fine—"

"—the horse thief said as they slipped the noose around his neck."

"Ray, I'm innocent," I protest.

"What's that got to do with it? We're talking about the criminal justice system here in L.A."

"Go with the Wagners. I can take care of myself."

I think I hear suppressed laughter on the other end of the line. Irritably I thank Ray for the heads up and tell him I am returning to the dinner table to finish my meal. Before he can respond, I hang up. First thing tomorrow I am going to have a chat with Detective Second Grade Huge Schapp and then I am going to track down Pete Rodriguez in Chula Vista and put a stop to this nonsense. I don't care whose birthday he's celebrating.

The next morning I'm out of the house by nine-thirty. I've told Bunny I'll be attending a hush-hush meeting of higher ups in the Writers Guild to talk about a strike later in the year. She accepts this because she knows we writers talk strike on a weekly basis though we seldom do anything about it. In any case I'll be free to nose around in the Wagner situation without arousing Bunny's avowed curiosity. Despite my promise to Bunny I have no intention of leaving the Wagners to the ineptitude of the L.A. judicial system.

It's a quick drive to the Van Nuys division, quick but fruitless. Schapp is working a case in Granada Hills. No telling when he will report back to headquarters. I ask the desk sergeant if he can give me Pete Rodriguez's temporary contact number in Chula Vista. He apologizes but he cannot. I say it's personal. Same reply. I tell him I want to confess to a notorious axe murder that took place on Halloween four years ago in Reseda. The sergeant, whose name is Duffy, knows me all too well and laughs out loud. So far this day has been very unproductive. I am 0 for 2 and about to try for a triple.

The Marquis Manor Inn is a fourth rate motel located on Century Boulevard on the outskirts of Inglewood near the airport. It suffers from dry rot, bedbugs and delusions of grandeur. It boasts 16 ground level units and 16 parking spots, two of which are occupied. These are either clueless tourists or locals enjoying a low cost ten-in-the-morning nooner. A sign promoting a.m. and p.m. room rates has only encouraged them.

The desk clerk's name is Waldo. I know because it's stitched on the pocket of his shirt followed by a red exclamation point. However, upon closer examination I discover that the punctuation is actually a ketchup stain.

"Miss Toms. That one," he says in disgust, pursing his lips. Waldo is on the tall side, chubby and balding. His eyelashes flutter a lot when he speaks.

"Which unit?" I ask. "I need to speak with her."

"Doesn't everyone?" Waldo observes.

"Meaning?"

"Meaning early this morning a lackey of the law appeared hoping to corner Miss Toms and I will tell you what I told him. Sometime last night under cover of darkness, she and her boyfriend or whatever he was supposed to be, left the premises stiffing me for a night's room rent."

"Destination?"

"Not a clue."

"What can you tell me about the boyfriend?" I ask.

"And who do I look like, information central?"

I smile and lay a twenty on the counter. He hesitates, then deftly palms it and slips it into his trouser pocket.

"She called him Dylan. I never got a last name. Just short of six feet, wavy auburn hair, milky pale blue eyes, superb eyelashes. More my type than hers but maybe that's just my hormones talking. Anything else?"

"I'd like to take a look around her room, that is, if you haven't yet rented it out."

Waldo smiles.

"I'm getting vibes that President Jackson is feeling lonely in my pants pocket and is in need of company. "

I dig out another twenty and slide it across the counter. Waldo slides me the key to number 6.

"I presume housekeeping has not yet gotten to the room."

"You presume correctly."

"You're sure?"

"Housekeeping is my good friend Linus who is still in bed and never rouses himself until noon at the earliest."

"Thank you," I say.

"De nada," he responds with a wispy smile.

I reach in my wallet for a business card which I hand him.

"In case you hear from either of them, let me know."

"And you will come running with more engravings of President Jackson?"

"You bet," I say.

The wispy smile broadens as he slips my card into his shirt pocket.

Unit 6 is cramped, musty, dimly lit and a litterbug's wet dream. Sheets and blankets have been tossed everywhere. Ditto some magazines and the remnants of takeout food from some local deli. I search the closet and rifle the drawers of the dresser and the nightstands. Nothing. I peek into the wastebaskets. More nothing and then I spot it next to the baseboard behind one of the baskets. I pick it up. It's a receipt from a parking lot and it only takes a moment to recognize the address. It's Pedro's Park-It, the lot across the street from Regal King Productions, and it's dated two days ago. Curiouser and curiouser. It sounds like it's time to have a talk with Gerhardt Koenig or, at the very least, his charming receptionist, the lovely Rosalie from Reseda.

Twenty minutes later, I pull into the lot. I'm not sure Pedro recognizes me but he remembers my oddball car so he throws me a smile of welcome. We get to chatting and I bring the conversation around to Marigold Toms whom I describe in detail. He draws a blank until I suggest she probably went into the building across the street and then it comes back to him. Yes, he remembers. Two days ago. She was in the building less than ten minutes when she came out, she was very annoyed, very unhappy. She was even less happy when Pedro reminded her of the five dollar minimum. Words were exchanged. Acrimony filled the air. Finally they settled on two dollars and the woman drove away, still in a foul mood. Pedro got the impression it was because of something that happened, or perhaps didn't happen, in the office building. I decide to find out for myself.

Happily Rosalie remembers me and I suspect it has a lot to do with my virile Mediterranean good looks. Yes, she also remembers the woman, a tiny little foul mouthed bitch who talked funny. She was looking for Mr. Cummings and when she learned that he was elsewhere she demanded to see Mr. King. He, too, was unavailable.

"I asked her what she wanted to see him about. She sneered and said it was none of my business," Rosalie says. "Well, I don't care if I am only a receptionist, people can't talk to me that way so I told her if she couldn't share the reason for her wanting to see him, I just wouldn't tell him she'd come to the office and of course, this made her real mad and finally she splutters something about him not having the rights to the book which is when she marched out slamming the door. A very rude person in my estimation."

I try for a little more information but Rosalie has no more to give and soon I am walking out onto the sidewalk, my mind a rat's nest of connections that I can't sort out. Marigold Toms is the daughter of someone named Prunella that Cummings was almost married to but not quite and now she is lying ill in a hospice bed after being abandoned by Cummings who is in Los Angeles with a contract to write a screenplay which he really doesn't know how to do and anyway he seems to have been far more interested in running down Marian Wagner with his car than sitting at a typewriter. As for Garrison King he was on the brink of getting screwed before Cummings was conveniently murdered and meanwhile Marigold showed up on location trying to get to Robert Wagner, God knows why, and further, she shows up at King's offices babbling about the film rights to the book which may or may not be in doubt and maybe King is going to get screwed after all.

I cross the street to the parking lot, all the time asking myself what Sam August would do in a situation like this, aside from bedding the nearest available female, and I cannot come up with a suitable answer. Now I ask you, what's the point of having a brilliant alter ego if you can't depend upon him in a pinch?

I'm a block from the house when I realize that a shiny new Lincoln town car is parked at my curb. I pull into the driveway and park by the kitchen entrance, then walk around front for a closer look. I'm not exactly a hermit but unexpected company is near the top of my list of no-no's. Then I spot Curly Baxter all decked out in his chauffeur's livery sitting behind the wheel reading today's 'Morning Telegraph'. He spots me and waves. I wave back and then open the front door. Jack Warner has come calling.

CHAPTER EIGHT

He's sitting in the living room, a magazine in his lap and a cold drink in his right hand. He looks up when I enter and smiles, raising his glass in a silent toast.

"That Irish gal of yours, Joe. She's all right. Makes a mean vodka tonic. Better hang onto her."

"Couldn't survive without her, Jack, and it's good to see you. Been too damned long."

"Agreed," he says sipping from his glass and laying the magazine aside.

"Is this social or otherwise?" I ask.

"A little of each," he replies.

Just then Bridget appears in the archway leading to the dining room and kitchen.

"I thought I heard the car, sir. Could I be in the way of fixing you something, sir?"

"Cold Coors, Bridget, thanks. And just bring the bottle."

"I will, sir. And you, sir?" she asks Warner.

"I'm fine, thank you," he replies.

She scurries off and I plop down in an easy chair.

"I can't remember the last time you were here at the house, Jack."

"Two years ago. The kid's tenth birthday. I brought her a stuffed

Bugs Bunny."

"She's still got it."

"Well, good for me, then," he says.

"So is it true, what I've been hearing? That you're quitting ?"

"Not exactly. Selling some shares."

"How many?"

"All of them."

"Who's the lucky buyer?"

"Seven Arts."

"Ray Stark."

"That's right."

"You could do worse."

"I know."

"But you're not stepping down."

"Not right away."

"Good," I say. "Sounds sinful. Warner Bros. without Jack Warner."

Bridget returns with my beer. I thank her and take a swig. It tastes good.

"I needed to talk to you, Joe," Warner says. " I could have called but then it occurred to me that I hadn't seen you in months. So here I am."

"I'm flattered," I say.

"You should be, bubala. I also haven't seen my brother Al in months but him I phone."

I love Jack Warner. Everybody else he calls schmuck, schmoe and schlemiel. Me he calls bubala which roughly translated is Yiddish for "dear one" or "beloved friend". It also means that Jack wants something. I know him all too well.

"So, Joe," he says, "tell me all about your friend, Garrison King."

"He's hardly my friend, Jack."

"He says otherwise or else I never would have met with him."

"He's a nickel and dime producer who wants me to write a screenplay for him at below minimum."

"The Enchanted Palazzo, a crappy book which my wife Ann read a few years back. Dreck from cover to cover. He wants me to distribute the film."

"He aims high."

"He also wants me to eat half what he paid for the rights."

"Nine dollars and forty cents?"

"Two hundred big ones."

"Two hundred dollars?" I manage in sham disbelief.

"He's on the hook for two hundred thousand."

I gasp, this time in genuine disbelief.

"I suppose he told you who he had signed to play the lead," Warner says.

"He did," I say. "Kinda hard to believe."

"Not if you know the babe the way I do and I was there at her christening as a courtesy to her father even though he made most of his pictures for Fox." Warner shakes his head. "Mike Curtiz says she should quit the film business and become a bell ringer for the Salvation Army during the holidays. That's how fuzzy-brained her priorities are."

"Well, if it makes you feel any better, King is scamming me as much as he is you."

"Yeah, I thought it might be something like that," Warner says, getting to his feet. I do likewise.

"Why don't you stay for dinner, Jack? I know Bunny'd love to see you."

"Can't. Ann's conned me into going over to the Zanucks tonight for barbecue and to meet some inner city preacher looking for some of that good movie money to help support his soup kitchen."

He looks me in the eye and shakes my hand warmly.

"Thanks for everything, Joe. You were the best. Still are. I can't say that about many people."

"That goes two ways, Jack."

"And if you and Mirisch are looking for a home for the Sam August picture, you know my number."

"I'm pretty sure he's hooked into UA."

"Fuck UA," Jack growls and then claps me affectionately on the shoulder as I walk him to the door.

"What are you going to do about Garrison King?" I ask.

"Fuck him, too. I'm getting tired, Joe. Real tired. Tired of the chiselers and the braggarts and the no-nothings but hell, they've always been around. I think it's the young hot shots sniffing around, ready to put me in the ground alongside Mayer and Cohn and Zukor. We made this town, God damn it. These pip-squeaks think they have all the answers. Hell, Joe, they can't even get the questions straight."

With that he goes out. I may see him again now and then but this is our goodbye and we both know it. I move to the window and watch as he shuffles down the walkway to his car. He's moving slowly and he's slightly stooped and I realize I'm watching another moment in the changing of the guard. Perhaps the last moment. He's right. None but Jack are left. Mayer, Zukor, Cohn, Fox, Laemmle, all dead. The new kids on the block are in charge. Maybe that's the way it should be but an age is passing and I try to convince myself that things are better. They aren't. For every Walter Mirisch there are a dozen Garrison Kings scratching for a piece of the action. I am very grateful that Sam August and I have discovered each other. Sam will never use me, abuse me, or betray me.

Cosmo calls about six. He's shown the photo of Horatio Cummings to Joshua Donen and the youngster has identified him as the man behind the wheel of the car. No surprise but now we can really concentrate on the circumstances of his death. In Pete Rodriguez's absence, Hugo Schapp is flailing around blindly, following me wherever I go, convinced, I suppose, that I am involved.

What worries me is what will happen if and when I convince him that I had nothing to do with the man's death. Logically he will then turn his attention to the Wagners which is totally absurd but he can do a lot of damage stomping around cluelessly. The press will be aroused, scandal will dominate the news, the Wagners will be hounded by third rate reporters feasting on sensationalism and meanwhile the real killer has a good chance of escaping justice in the cloud of confusion created by Schapp's ineptitude. I make a mental note to camp out at the Van Nuys station tomorrow morning until I can reach Pete Rodriguez and convince him to call off his junkyard dog.

I needn't have worried. At 9:05 the next morning, my phone rings.

"Joe?"

"Pete?"

"My office. Ten o'clock. Don't be late or I'll send a squad car to drag you here in cuffs."

He hangs up. Something tells me this will not be a red letter day.

Pete Rodriguez looks up from a pile of paperwork on his desk and fixes me with a beady stare as I walk into his office.

"My father-in-law is celebrating his birthday this afternoon with friends, family and neighbors. I am not there as you can see. When I last saw her my wife was not speaking to me. For this I have you to thank. Sit down, Joe, and don't speak until I tell you to."

Chastened I sit down in the chair opposite his desk, hands in lap, while he returns to his paperwork. Minutes pass and finally he lays his pencil down and stares at me.

"Do you remember a conversation we had when last we met?"

"I do."

"Then maybe you can explain why you have been driving all over town, from that movie production office to the Beverly Hills Police to that moth-eaten motel on Century Boulevard."

"Trying to tie up some loose ends," I say.

"Or cover your tracks? Or intimidate people who might involve you in the death of this guy Cummings?"

"Bullshit."

"Are you aware that you are suspect number one in this murder?"

"According to who? Your feeble-minded partner?"

"All you need to make the grade is motive, means and opportunity and you qualify on all counts."

"Motive? What would that be?" I ask in annoyance.

"Not totally sure but I believe it has something to do with the actor Robert Wagner. Feel free to disagree."

That momentarily shuts me up as I rack my brain trying to figure how and where I slipped up.

"Where'd you get that idea?" I ask lamely, afraid to hear the answer.

"Marigold Toms."

"You caught up with her."

"And not a moment too soon, no thanks to you. She was getting ready to board a BOAC jetliner to Belfast when we grabbed her. Got a tip from Al Hoffman over at the Beverly Hills police. You'd mentioned my name."

"You're holding her. On what charge?"

"Disturbing the peace."

"At the location."

"That's right."

"You can't hold her for long."

"I know that but I wasn't about to let her flee the jurisdiction before I found out what the hell was going on."

"Can I speak with her?"

He gives me a look of total incredulity.

"Joe, you have the attention span of an oyster. Maybe you'd like to call Bunny and the two of you can question her together."

"No, no, forget it," I say quickly.

"I thought so. I haven't ratted you out yet, Joe, but don't tempt me," Pete says.

"Meaning what?"

"Meaning she's called me twice, making me promise to let her know if you suddenly start playing Dick Tracy again."

"Okay. Forget I asked."

"Anyway, you know what we know. It was all in that correspondence. Cummings ditched Marigold's ailing mother to come to L.A. to write the movie."

"And Marigold followed him here because?"

"She didn't say but I got the distinct impression she had no use for the guy, none whatsoever."

"Makes her a mighty likely suspect," I suggest.

Pete nods. "You would think."

"What about the boyfriend? Where's he?"

He looks at me sharply. I've caught him by surprise.

"Boyfriend? What boyfriend?" he asks.

"Dylan somebody. Also Irish. Maybe English. I got the feeling they were joined at the hip the moment they hit town."

"You're sure about this?"

"You haven't checked out the Marquis Manor."

"Not yet."

"Talk to Waldo, the desk clerk. He's bubbling over with information. Marigold and Dylan shared the premises and were undoubtedly sexually intimate though Waldo would prefer to believe otherwise. You might ask her what she's doing here in L.A. before some two buck lawyer gets her out on a habeas and clams her up."

He stares at me momentarily, then shouts for his partner. A moment later Hugo Schapp appears in the doorway, throwing me a dirty look.

"Yeah, Sarge?" he says.

"That British Airways flight that the babe was going to take back to Belfast. Call the airline, find out if they had a passenger on that flight, first name Dylan, NLN."

"Right," he says, ducking out. Pete turns his attention back to me.

"Marigold Toms is tied to Wagner by virtue of her intrusion onto the movie set. She's tied to Horatio Cummings because of the correspondence found in his luggage. By me, this ties Wagner to Cummings who is very much dead at the hands of person or persons unknown but certainly not a run of the mill mugger. Am I making sense?"

"It's a stretch," I lie, hoping to divert him up a different alley. "More likely is some sort of involvement with a guy named Garrison King for whom Cummings death was a gift from God."

"And Garrison King is?" Pete queries.

"A ragamuffin movie producer whose troubles ended when Cummings breathed his last." I give him King's address and fill in King's dilemma, suggesting that Pete check into King's activities quickly and thoroughly.

He nods.

"I'm going to do that, Joe. Me. The detective in charge of the case, the one the city of Los Angeles pays to deal with these situations. Not you, private citizen and well known buttinsky. You stay out of this. You go home and sit down at your typewriter and go back to work on your latest book because if you don't, friend or no friend, I will pick up the phone and call Bunny because your wife and I have one thing in common, we want to see you live to a ripe old age that permits you to enjoy your grandchildren. Do I make myself clear?"

I hesitate, then nod, knowing I have no choice. Wagner has already asked me to disappear, now Pete Rodriguez and if Bunny is ever brought into it, I am dead meat.

"Sarge!" Hugo Schapp appears in the doorway. "You had it

nailed," he says. "Guy's name is Pfieffer. Dylan Pfieffer. I have an address in Belfast which I think is in Ireland."

Pete nods.

"Call the authorities. Have someone check to make sure he actually made it all the way home."

"Right."

"Also anything else we ought to know about the guy."

"Okay."

He starts to go, Pete stops him.

"And Hugo. You can stop following Mr. Bernardi all around town. He is not a suspect in this case."

Schapp frowns. "You sure about that, Sarge?" he asks.

"Very sure. Now call the Irish cops."

Schapp gives me one more suspicious look and then disappears. I look over at Pete who is also giving me the fisheye.

"Thanks," I say with a smile. "Now that I'm just a bystander, how about a couple of minutes with Marigold."

"You don't give up, do you?"

"Curiosity, Pete. Curiosity, that's all."

"Fine. Sooner or later we're going to have to ship her off to a judge who undoubtedly will send her on her way with a fine and a warning. That'll be your big chance to pump her for her life story."

"Pete—"

"Go home, Joe. Go to your office. Write your book."

"Right," I say, getting to my feet. Except for the fact that Walter Mirisch and I may lose Bob Wagner for the movie, I actually feel a bit of relief. What film was it in which the aging action hero said, I'm getting too old for this shit? My sentiments exactly.

CHAPTER NINE

Friday morning. Two days have passed since my dressing down from Pete Rodriguez. I have figuratively chained myself to my desk, laboring over 'The Ill Mannered Diplomat' and having nothing to do with Robert Wagner, Cosmo Stryker, Pete Rodriguez, Marigold Toms or anyone else remotely connected to the death of Horatio Cummings. I would like to say that Cummings' murder has completely escaped my mind. I would like to say it but I can't. My brain is constantly drifting from fiction into unresolved real life mayhem and I suddenly realize as I look at my pages that I have painted myself into a corner from which there is no escape. This is the price I pay for not obliterating Cummings from my psyche.

I have stripped Sam down to his skivvies, locked him in the upper floor of an abandoned warehouse overlooking the Seine, chained him to a wall, and released hungry rats on the ground floor who have already picked up the scent of the pork fat I have slavered all over Sam's body. Dawn LaRue is aboard the night train to Orleans to recover the secret plans from the safe in Sikorsky's villa. With no one around to rescue him, Sam is a goner unless I can come up with some credible escape plan which I now realize I can't do without turning this latest adventure into a comic book. I ask myself, what would Ian Fleming do? It doesn't help.

I am too stubborn to admit defeat so I sharpen a dozen pencils. That doesn't help either. That's when the phone rings and I pick up gratefully. I need diversion. It's Walter.

"Did I catch you at a bad time?" he asks.

"Not really," I reply. "I'm blocked."

"Happens to the best. Izzy Diamond was stuck on the ending for 'Some Like It Hot', sat in front of his typewriter one day for nine straight hours before the perfect tag line came too him."

"Nobody's perfect."

"Precisely. Don't worry about it, Joe. What do you hear from Bob Wagner?"

"Nothing. For now he's off my radar. Bunny has laid down the law."

"I understand. I haven't given up on him but just to be on the safe side I've checked out a couple of new names."

"Shoot."

"Tab Hunter."

"Get serious."

"I know. It's my brother Marvin's idea and I promised I'd bring him up."

"Did you check out George Segal?" I ask.

"Committed to 'The St Valentine's Day Massacre."

"Steve McQueen?"

"More trouble than he's worth," Walter says. "George Peppard?"

"All the warmth of the Titanic iceberg."

"I do have one other thought but I doubt you've heard of him."

"Try me," I say.

"Jack Nicholson."

I'm rendered speechless.

"You mean 'Hells Angels on Wheels' Jack Nicholson? 'Back Door to Hell' Jack Nicholson? Those two and a bunch of other shit movies, maybe some unreleasable. Walter, he's not the hero, he is not the friend of the hero, he's not even a friend of the friend?" In casting parlance this means he is a nonentity, the third guy through the door.

"I think you're wrong, Joe. He's got something."

"I hope it's not contagious."

"Very funny."

"Walter, if you're that hot to go with a nobody, we might as well roll the dice with Eastwood."

"Too late," Walter says. "He just signed with Universal to star in 'Coogan's Bluff'. I'm told his character has lots of polysyllabic dialogue."

"Okay, okay so I'm a schmuck. Let's hang in with Wagner a while longer. Maybe this thing will sort itself out."

"I'm game if you are."

"Deal."

"Deal."

I hang up the phone convinced that I am involved in a film that never will be, not an unusual occurrence in this city of broken dreams. The phone rings. I pick up. Another of Walter's suggestions, no doubt.

"Who now?" I ask.

"Who now what?" comes a voice I recognize instantly.

"Ray?"

"Yeah Ray. Your favorite lawyer. Have you been drinking?

"Maxwell House," I reply. "Three cups so far. My nervous system is starting to bitch. What's new?"

"Nothing good. Cosmo called to tell me Wagner's been invited by Rodriguez to the Van Nuys station to chat about Horatio Cummings."

"Shit," I murmur to myself.

"I agree," Ray says. "I'll be there, of course. I'm just calling to see if there's anything you know that I ought to know."

"I don't think so. I've been gently advised by my wife to mind my own business."

"So I hear. Do you want a detailed rundown of what occurs at the meeting or are you permanently pussy whipped?"

"Crude, Ray. Very crude."

"I know," he says. "You didn't answer the question."

"I'll be here at my desk all day," I say.

"I'll get back to you."

He hangs up and I lean back in my chair, staring at my framed poster for 'Lawrence of Arabia' and wishing that Peter O'Toole was not so old and not so Irish. And even as I think it, I dismiss the thought. For weeks I have envisioned Bob Wagner as Sam August. He's in the forefront of my brain as I write the scenes. I'm now at the point where no one else will do any more than Lee Marvin could replace Basil Rathbone as Sherlock Holmes. My gaze shifts to the lonely sheet of paper in my typewriter. Sam chained to the wall, rats on the march, and in the real world, R.J. Wagner about to be grilled by Pete Rodriguez. And then as I stare a thought comes to me and I get up from my desk and hurry downstairs. I grab my car keys and am heading out the door when Bridget intercepts me. If the lady of the house calls, where should she say I've gone? I smile and tweak Bridget under her chin. A job interview, I say. Somebody wants to hire me.

Rosalie, the receptionist, looks up with a smile as I walk through the door. I'm flattered that she recognizes me, then realize that she thinks I'm Garrison King's accountant. I reintroduce myself and ask for the man himself. She says she will see if he's available and buzzes the intercom. A moment later she tells me to walk right in and points to King's door.

I find him at his desk drinking coffee and eating a bagel and smearing cream cheese all over a script he has been trying to read.

I glimpse the title as he tosses it aside. 'Batwomen from the Planet Zircon'.

"Trash," he says grumpily before he breaks into a smile for my benefit. "The photograph of Mr. Cummings? It was useful?"

"Very."

"I'm pleased."

"Have you found a screenwriter for Horatio's novel yet?" I ask.

"I have feelers out. Mr. Rod Serling has expressed interest."

In his dreams, I think to myself.

"I've reconsidered, Mr. King," I say. "I'm available if you are still interested."

His smile broadens.

"But of course I am interested. Although it is a handsome fee I confess I might have been able to make it more had you won that Oscar but, well, that is no longer of consequence, is it? Perhaps this script will be your leap into the upper tier of your profession."

I smile. I should be so lucky.

"For me, Mr. King, it is not so much about the money but the work itself. The journey, not the destination."

"Excellent." The smile has not left his face. "You will understand that I am unable to offer you points but I see that is of no consequence to you." Points are percentages of the profits. To get them writers have been known to sell off their young.

"I expected no profit participation," I say, "but I would like to be certain that this picture will be made."

"It will be, I assure you," King says.

"Then there's no cloud on the rights due to Mr. Cummings unfortunate demise?"

"None."

"Good. I'd like to satisfy myself about that. Do you have a copy of your agreement with Mr. Cummings."

The smile fades. He eyes me suspiciously, then reaches in a desk draper and pulls out a manila envelope which he hands me.

"I have nothing to hide, Mr. Bernardi," he says.

I slip the contract from the envelope and the first thing I notice is the letterhead. "Dylan Pfieffer & Associates, Solicitors. 277 Cliftonville Road, Belfast, No. Ireland." Another player emerges. Marigold Toms' traveling companion is more than just a bed partner. Cummings' death is now starting to assume the complexity of a thousand piece jigsaw puzzle.

"Dylan Pfieffer," I say aloud.

"Yes."

"The solicitor."

"Yes."

"When was the last time you saw him?" I ask.

"I didn't," King says.

"You didn't?"

"No, everything was done by mail."

"And you didn't see him in the past few days?"

"How could I?"

"He's been here in Los Angeles for the past week or so."

"No."

"Yes."

"How strange."

"And he didn't contact you, come by for a chat, meet you somewhere for a schnapps?"

"I told you, I've never met him," King says, annoyance beginning to show.

"Or Marigold Toms?"

"Whoever that is," he says with a shrug.

Just then I spot a book lying on the corner of King's desk. I pick it up. Lucky me. It's a copy of 'The Enchanted Palazzo'. I get to my feet.

"I'm going to take these home and read them both over tonight.

Tomorrow I'll return and we can discuss the screenplay."

"Sorry. I can't permit you to take the contract from this office, Mr. Bernardi."

"Do you have a Xerox machine?"

"Yes, but Miss Birnbaum has not yet deciphered the operating instructions?"

I raise my eyes to heaven. She's probably just as handy with a pencil sharpener.

"Show me where it is," I sigh.

I had planned to drive straight home but as lunch hour was nearing I walk down to the corner cafe where I first ran into Horatio Cummings and order a sausage sandwich and a Coors. My doctors would not approve. At the moment I don't care. I read while I eat.

The contract drawn up by Dylan Pfieffer is pretty straightforward. For $25,000 King has obtained a one year option to the rights to 'The Enchanted Palazzo'. In the event the movie is actually made, an additional $175,000 will be due and payable upon completion of principal photography. It further stipulates that Horatio Cummings will write the screenplay for an additional payment of $50,000. In the event that Cummings is replaced as the film's writer, the contract for the rights to the book becomes immediately null and void. I give Pfieffer a silent salute of approval. Even though he is an Irish Brit, he has written the contract so that even an American layman can understand it and though I am no lawyer, it seems tamperproof to me. In the unlikely event of Cummings' demise the payment for the rights becomes part of his estate and it is King's good fortune that the estate doesn't demand to write the screenplay. I think to myself, how could King have been so lucky? How indeed, I ask myself suspiciously. Tonight I will speed read enough of the book to discuss it intelligently and tomorrow Garrison King and I will meet to plot out the film scenario. I will also pump King about his dealings with Cummings. I am pretty sure there's a lot to dig up. Maybe enough to clear the Wagners of any involvement in Cummings' death.

I head for home. On the way here and now on the way back to the house, I see no sign of Detective Second Class Hugo Schapp. Pete's intervention has called him off. I am relieved. I am less relieved when Bunny arrives home just before supper and listens to my story with outright skepticism.

"You said the book was garbage," she says.

"It is, but I'm having trouble with the new novel and it's also a nice piece of change for not much work so I thought I'd give it a fling."

"Horse puckey," she says. For Bunny, this is an outright obscenity.

"You scoff at money?"

"We don't need the money."

"No? Listen, gorgeous. Me Tarzan, you Jane. Me hunt, put meat on the table. You sit by the fire and mend socks."

"Oh, brother," she says, raising her eyes to heaven.

"Look, I'm bored, it's a challenge so I'm going to have a crack at it."

"And it has nothing to do with Horatio Cummings death?"

"Of course not," I say with the straightest face I can conjure up.

"We'll see," she says obviously not believing a word I say.

From there things get worse. We're in the middle of dinner when the phone rings. Bridget peers in from the doorway to tell me Ray Giordano is on the phone. He says the call is important. I hesitate, then say I'll take it in the library. I look over at Bunny who gives me the fisheye. Oh, what a tangled web we weave—.

Ray tells me the meeting at the Van Nuys station with Pete Rodriguez did not go well. Advised to tell the truth, the Wagners did just that. Yes, Marian knew Cummings some years back in London. He was a casual acquaintance she'd met at a cocktail party. When pressed she'd admitted she was annoyed by him, then confirmed that he had stalked her. Her husband at the time, Stanley Donen, forcefully put a stop to it. Somehow the press got hold of it. For several days it was page one in the tabloids with Cummings labeled a sick pervert, then the story faded away. The picture wrapped, the Donens returned to the States and that was the end of it, or so it seemed. Several weeks ago the stalking and harassment resumed anonymously. Marian had no doubt who was behind it and confided in her now husband, Robert Wagner. Cosmo Stryker was hired to provide protection. Then several days later Marian was nearly killed in the hit-and-run attempt. Because unwanted publicity might ensue, the police were not brought into it.

"So what do you think?" I ask.

"I think Rodriguez is not satisfied. He's going to keep digging," Ray says.

"What about Marigold Toms? What did he say about her?"

"Nothing and I didn't ask."

"Is he still holding her?"

"I doubt it. Even a public defender would have her out by now if a judge hadn't already kicked her loose. Trespassing onto a movie set, that's a pretty low level beef, Joe."

"Yeah," I mutter.

"Come on, Joe. I know you're worried but look on the bright side. You know Pete Rodriguez, he's a straight arrow. He honestly thinks he has something here and he won't get off the Wagners until he can prove to himself they weren't involved."

I sigh. I am disappointed but not devastated. At age 46 I have seen enough of life to know that it kicks you in the groin at the most inopportune times. Nonetheless I must do what must be done and so I immediately call Pete Rodriguez.

"I thought you'd be calling," he says when he comes on the line.

"Pete, believe me, the Wagners had nothing to do with your homicide," I say.

"Maybe not."

"But if their names get leaked to the press, it could be devastating not only to Marian Wagner but to the two boys as well, all sorts of innuendo splashed across the front page, being hounded by callous reporters who care about nothing but a story—"

"I get it, Joe, and I'm going to keep their names out of it for as long as I can—"

"I appreciate that, Pete, but leaks happen—"

"They won't happen on my end. Now, at the risk of repeating myself, butt out, old buddy."

"Yeah, I know. Calm down, write your book, and come see me when you've graduated from the police academy."

"Something like that."

Click. He's gone.

I know that this moment will pass, that the Wagners will be exonerated, and that Wagner will be on to other things. This is not a tragedy in the big scheme of things and that, if I'm lucky, in a few months a movie will be in production and I will hardly remember this phone call at all. If I'm not lucky Sam August will be collecting dust in Walter Mirisch's office and Robert Wagner will be hogtied to some godawful television series. Those being the alternatives, I decide I cannot rely on luck to solve this problem.

CHAPTER TEN

By the next morning I have it all worked out. Mentally and emotionally I am committed to Bob Wagner and I am deathly afraid that Walter will call and tell me that Audie Murphy is available. Of course he won't. Walter is a lot smarter than that but I don't want to hear any more about alternatives and if I have to defy my wife and Pete Rodriguez and Ray Giordano, I am determined to cast Wagner as Sam August. This means I need a plan that will not only be productive but one I can execute in deep shadows. An idea came to me last night while I was sleeping and it is still germinating in my brain. It is predicated on the premise that Marigold Toms was brought before a magistrate and was either freed outright or put on probation.

The cops and the courts are within spitting distance of one another at the Van Nuys Civic Center and after I drive into the parking lot, I avoid confronting my buddy Pete Rodriguez and go in search of another old friend, Casey Krumholz, chief clerk of the municipal court. Casey and I go back seven or eight years when he tipped me to the whereabouts of a grandmotherly klepto who had been robbing the May Company blind for years, despite the best efforts of the District Attorney, the court system and a half dozen probation officers to stop her. I find him in the cafeteria drinking coffee and munching on a prune Danish.

"Who's minding the store?" I smile down at him, a mug of black coffee in my hand.

He looks up and smiles back.

"Penny Waters. I spell her at eleven and how are you doing, Joe? Been a while."

"Busy busy, Casey."

I sit down and sip the brew. It's plenty hot and I yelp when I burn my tongue. Casey laughs.

"They keep it that way to disguise the rancid taste," he says. Casey's a wizened little fella, no taller than five foot three with close cropped white hair, weighs maybe a hundred and ten pounds soaking wet and wears thick lensed tortoise shell glasses. "And whom are we trying to track down today, Joe?"

"It didn't occur to you that this might be a social call?"

"Not for a second. What's the beef this time and who's the beefee?"

"Murder," I say, "but what I need from you is small potatoes. Also something of a long shot."

"Wow. Two cliches in one sentence and you call yourself a writer?"

"Sorry," I say.

"Well, who cares. Murders intrigue me. Proceed," he says, squashing a pat of butter into his Danish.

"Sometime in the last two or three days a woman might have appeared in front of the judge on a trespass charge. Name's Marigold Toms."

"I remember her," Casey says. "Little bit of a thing. British."

"That's her, " I reply.

"She's got a guy with her, claims to be her lawyer but he's a barrister or some such in Ireland. The judge tells him to sit down and shut up. He fines the woman a hundred bucks and gives her ninety days probation. She starts for my desk but the lawyer guy is way ahead of her handing me five twenties. I ask for an address and she looks kind of blank which is when the lawyer guy says she'll be staying at the Biltmore."

"I don't suppose you got his name."

"The lawyer? Nah. What for? So what do you think, Joe? She knocked some guy off or what?"

"Don't know, Casey. Gotta talk to her first."

"Let me know how it works out," Casey says.

"Will do," I say and then make the mistake of asking him about his six grandchildren. Thirty minutes later I'm walking out to the parking lot, a distinct buzzing sound echoing in my ears.

The Biltmore is a crown jewel among Los Angeles' hotels, greatly favored by both the elite and nouveaux riche wannabes. If Marigold and her lawyer buddy, Dylan Pfieffer, are staying there, it's a far cry from the Marquis Manor. A puzzlement. And the other puzzlement is the presence of Pfieffer back in L.A. after spending only two or three days in Belfast.

I walk through the lobby toward the registration desk and am immediately disappointed not to see Lance, my favorite desk clerk. On the few occasions when I have nosed around this august place in search of information, Lance has been unfailingly cooperative. It hasn't taken a discreet twenty dollar bill either, merely a gleam in Lance's eye that yearned for moments to come that never materialized. To his credit Lance has never given up.

I have two choices. One's a beady-eyed bald guy with a pencil-thin mustache. I decide to wait for the cute redhead with the pageboy hairdo. She smiles as I approach the desk. Her name tag reads Cynthia.

"Good morning, sir," she says. "Checking in?"

"Actually I'm here to visit a friend. Marigold Toms."

"Toms. Toms," she mutters to herself as she consults a register, then shakes her head. "Sorry, sir, we have no one named Toms registered."

I nod.

"How about Pfieffer? Dylan Pfieffer?"

She checks again. More muttering.

"Yes, Mr. Pfieffer is one of our guests."

"Excellent," I say.

"He checked in early yesterday morning. Strange there's no notation that he would be sharing the room."

"Yes, very strange," I say solemnly.

"Perhaps this Toms woman is his sister," the redhead posits without looking me in the eye.

"Or even a cousin," I say, starting to lose patience. "Look, Cynthia, I appreciate the fact that you are being circumspect but I am not the police and I don't care who is shacking up with whom or who knows about it. Now, may I have the room number? I'd like to surprise them."

"Sorry, sir, that's against policy. You may use the white courtesy phone on the wall and ask for your party. Our operator will be happy to connect you."

"That won't help the surprise much, will it?" I say turning up the charm to maximum.

"No, sir, I don't suppose it will," she says sweetly but firmly. And then, looking around furtively, she adds, "In any case, I don't believe they are in the room."

"Oh?"

"Now that my memory's been jogged I believe I saw her earlier in the lobby with Mr. Pfieffer. I heard they were on the way to a local department store to buy a black dress. Someone told our head of housekeeping that late last evening Miss Toms received news that her mother had died unexpectedly overseas. A stroke, I think. Maybe a heart attack. Apparently it was not unexpected but she was sketchy on the details."

"Tragic," I say.

"The concierge says she inquired about the availability of plane tickets back to Ireland. He's looking into it."

"How thoughtful of him," I say. "I don't suppose you know the name of the department store she went to."

"No, I don't, sir," the redhead says getting all huffy, "and even if I did,I couldn't help you. We here at the Biltmore are dedicated first and foremost to protecting the privacy of our guests."

"A very wise policy," I say with a nod. "Keep up the good work."

I exit the hotel and return to my car where I slip behind the steering wheel and for a few moments I sit in thoughtful silence. Again, I ask myself, who the hell is this Dylan Pfieffer and where does he fit into this picture? Fact. He drew up the contract between Horatio and Garrison King. Fact. He is also close to Marigold Toms who despised Cummings for the way he had abandoned her mother in her hour of need. Pretty much a fact. From what Waldo, the desk clerk at the cheesy motel had said, Pfieffer's relationship with Marigold was not restricted to legal advice. And then I remember that I promised King I would stop by to discuss the script in the broadest of strokes. Yes, that should be my next stop. For whatever reason King seems to be squarely in the middle of my conundrum and the right question asked in the right way might reveal something I need to know.

I drive to Regal King Productions hoping to find a parking spot on the street. I don't. My old pal Pedro smiles as I pull into his usurous parking lot. He remembers me. I remember the five dollars minimum and grumble to myself about it all the way into the building. Upstairs, I walk through the door to find Rosalie in a testy conversation with the power company about an unpaid bill that is two months in arrears. When she finally hangs up in frustration, Rosalie hits me with the bad news. King is not there, he is on location with his latest film. They are shooting in a pocket-sized picnic park in Encino. She gives me directions and I hurry back to

Pedro who smiles benignly and puts out his hand for the fiver. I was gone ten minutes, I protest. Fifty cents a minute, I wail. Pedro merely smiles. I truly believe that someday soon this man will own the entire city of Los Angeles.

I hustle over the hill into the Valley, pick up Victory Boulevard and then turn onto White Oak. The park should be dead ahead but I don't see the army of trucks and trailers associated with a location shoot. There's a white van owned by an auto parts store and a bunch of cars parked at curbside but that's it. Maybe I'm too late. Maybe Rosalie gave me the wrong address. A dozen or so families are using the barbecues and the picnic tables, tots are playing in the sandboxes, and the older kids are climbing all over the jungle gym or enjoying the swings. This makes no sense. This is supposed to be a school day.

I park some fifty yards away and start toward the park and that's when I catch sight of Garrison King leaning against that new Cadillac convertible watching intently. I am momentarily confused and then just at that moment a "thing" emerges from the forest which abuts the picnic area. I say "thing" because that's what it is, half-man, half-green lizard, bare chested and wearing little more than cut-off jeans to disguise his private parts. It screams, a piercing yowl designed to wake the dead and it has the desired effect. People scatter in fear, mothers race to protect their children, teenage girls run for cover. The thing darts toward the swings, waving it's scaly clawed arms menacingly. Pandemonium reigns. The thing upends a picnic table and then fiercely eyeing his surroundings looks for more mayhem to commit. Suddenly the shrill sound of a whistle fills the air. The thing immediately takes off on a dead run toward the white van. Someone inside throws open the rear doors and the thing jumps in and the van burns rubber leaving the scene. Immediately on its tail is Garrison King in his Cadillac. I race back to my Bentley to give chase.

Now as I follow King and his van through the streets of the Valley, it is all too clear to me what has just happened. King has 'stolen' a scene operating without a permit and filming unaware bystanders instead of hiring union-mandated extras. This is the lowest form of film-making, as unethical as it is illegal. A question pops to mind. Is Regal King Productions just cheap or is it broke? Whichever, I need to find out.

A few minutes later the van pulls into the parking lot at the rear of St. Mel's Church in Woodland Hills. Except for a couple of parish-owned cars the lot is empty. The van parks at the edge of the lot farthest from the church. King parks beside it and I'm close behind. As I'm getting out of my car, the doors to the van open and a young actor emerges carrying a wet towel and wiping away the last vestiges of the green makeup which had covered his body. A couple of others emerge from the van and they are joined by King. Conversation ensues. A moment later one of the men sees me approaching and says something. King sees me and his face turns dark. He steps toward me, takes my arm and moves me away from the others.

"I did not expect to see you out here in the Valley, Mr. Bernardi."

"Same for me, Mr. King. And you can relax, I think you've successfully evaded the police, at least for the moment."

"We have," he nods. "This sort of thing, working without a permit, I seldom engage in it but time was important and I couldn't wait around for the red tape and the approvals. Dealing with the authorities can be very trying."

"How well I know," I say. I nod toward the van. "The guy in green. He looks familiar but I can't place him."

"Nick Edrick. Gold medal winner in the last Olympics. Light heavyweight division wrestling. He thought his win would be his ticket to fame and fortune but the truth is, for the most part, the public doesn't give a damn about Olympic winners so when I offered

Nick the title role in 'Revenge of the Gila Monster' he jumped at it. If he clicks I've got him tied up for three more pictures."

"At a bargain basement salary, no doubt," I say.

He shrugs.

"Business is business. If it could happen to Mr. Weissmuller and Mr. Crabbe, it could happen to Mr. Edrick, but until it does I am the one taking the risk."

"Speaking of taking a risk, you and I have got to talk."

His face darkens.

"That sounds ominous."

"Let's find a place where we can chat without being interrupted," I suggest.

McCaffrey's is a quiet, dimly lit bar and grill on Ventura Blvd near the intersection with DeSoto Avenue. At this hour of the day, it is extremely quiet and dim approaching dark. Besides King and me there is one souse in the place, slouched over the bar nursing a beer and in danger of falling off his stool. King and I have slipped into a booth at the far end of the room where we can converse in private. I'm having my usual cold Coors, he's opted for a dark German ale I've never heard of.

"So, Mr. Bernardi, " King says, "we are seated and now you will tell me your problem."

"Dylan Pfieffer is back in town, staying at the Biltmore and don't tell me you haven't met."

"We haven't."

"Mr. King, either you want me to write your screenplay or you don't but if you continue to bullshit me, I'm going to get up from this booth, go out that door and you will never see me again."

"Mr. Pfieffer and I have spoken on the phone. Once. A courtesy call. He called to let me know he was in the city, that was all. I have never met the man face to face."

"Tell me, do you consider yourself a lucky man?"

"In what way?"

"A few days ago you were saddled with an untalented writer whose demands threatened to derail your million dollar deal. Then fate intervened and Horatio Cummings was shot and killed by person or persons unknown but definitely not a street mugger. I'd say that was either the best of luck or maybe something else."

"Something else? Meaning what, sir?"

"Figure it out," I tell him.

His eyes turn cold.

"Your suggestion is monstrous," he says.

"Is it?"

"At the time Mr. Cummings was accosted I was in a card game with a half dozen witnesses who will swear that I never left the table."

"Precisely what I would have arranged were I in your shoes," I tell him.

He starts to get up.

"I've had quite enough of this," he says.

I seize his arm and hold it down.

"Where did you get the money?" I ask.

"What money? What are you talking about?"

"I'm talking about the twenty five thousand in cash you paid to secure the option on the book. You can't even pay a piddling electric bill but still you managed to scrape up twenty five G's. At least that's what it says in the contract. Did any money actually change hands, Mr. King? Is that something I should ask Dylan Pfieffer about? Were you and Pfieffer involved in some sort of scam to defraud Mr. Cummings?"

"Absolutely not and I resent the accusation. I was able to borrow the money to seal our deal. There was no fraud."

"Borrow from who? What bank?"

"No bank. I dealt with a private individual."

"A loan shark."

"When the film goes forward I will have no trouble repaying the loan."

I shake my head.

"Incredible," I say. "You borrow twenty-five large from the likes of No Nose Shapiro or one of his associates and then realize you have no script and you will never have one as long as you're stuck with Horatio Cummings. And if you shitcan Cummings from the project, you no longer own the rights to the material so there you are, up the creek without a paddle and No Nose hassling you for his money back."

"It was a business arrangement. I was in no danger," King says.

"Maybe not in Dusseldorf. Here the game is played differently. By the way which of our upstanding citizens did you do business with?"

"I would rather not say," King says, not saying.

"Then tell me this," I say. "Did you happen to mention your dilemma to the gentleman?"

King hesitates, then shakes his head.

"That, too, is a subject I would rather not discuss," he says before draining the remains of his tankard of ale. "But I will tell you this, Mr. Bernardi. I had nothing to do with Horatio's death."

"Maybe yes, maybe no, but here's something you can count on. I am going to keep at it until I find the person who did."

CHAPTER ELEVEN

"What are you telling me? That the mob killed this queer novelist because, why? Because he was a lousy writer and couldn't write a screenplay? You make no sense."

For the past thirty minutes I have been trying to explain to Aaron Kleinschmidt how and why Horatio Cummings was killed in a phony back alley shooting staged to look like a stickup gone wrong. I'm having little luck.

"I told you, Aaron, Horatio Cummings was not a homosexual."

"And you know this how, from personal experience?"

"No, someone else's."

"But you won't say who."

"No, I won't. I can't. But the killer is a shylock and a big one, big enough to handle 25 Gs without raising a sweat."

"Doesn't narrow the field much," Aaron points out. "And need I remind you, my meddling friend, that shylocks seldom resort to murder, merely broken bones. Murder gets in the way of profit."

Aaron is a smart guy. He's a good friend. He also holds the rank of Inspector and heads the LAPD Homicide Bureau operating out of the Police Administration Building in downtown Los Angeles. There are times when he suffers from blind spots. This is one of them.

"Seldom is not never, Aaron. Maybe the shy wasn't getting his vig and realized King was flatter than a year old bottle of Pepsi. He goes after Horatio who now has the twenty-five large and who, not knowing how the game is played, does or says something really stupid—"

"Like he's going to go to the cops—"

"Yeah, like that. Anyway, it's not a stretch. Otherwise I kinda like King for it except that he has a seven man alibi and besides which, I don't think he has the balls."

"Nice theory," Aaron says, "but what are you telling me for? It's Pete Rodriguez's case. Tell him and get off my back."

"I can't."

"You can't?"

"He told me to butt out and if I didn't he was going to rat me out to Bunny."

Aaron's face breaks into a wide grin.

"All these years," he says, "why didn't I ever think of that? I may recommend Pete for promotion."

"Aw, come on, Aaron, you think I like this?"

"Actually, Joe, I think you do," Aaron says, suddenly becoming serious. "You're way past forty, much too old to keep playing cops and robbers. I can't believe you're still alive, the messes you get yourself into. But enough is enough and Bunny is right. One heart attack is more than enough for you so butt out of police business, go home and take care of your family."

"Aaron—"

"Not another word, Joe. Out, or so help me, I'll lock you up for the night."

I open my mouth and then wisely shut it. My tail between my legs I leave Aaron's office and take the elevator to the main floor. I am furious, choking on frustration. I'm pretty sure I know exactly what happened and I can't do a thing about it. Meanwhile, nothing has changed. Pete Rodriguez has a homicide to solve and protecting Marian Wagner's privacy is not a priority. If Lou Cioffi or some other eager beaver newshound learns of what came before, all hell will break loose. If I share with him everything I know, he'll drop a dime on me and all hell will break loose in the bedroom I share with my beloved Bunny.

I take Aaron's advice. I go home mostly because I am at a dead end and have nowhere else to go. I grab a Nehi from my mini fridge and sit down at my typewriter where I stare at the half finished page I abandoned hours earlier. Sam is still half naked, still covered with pork fat and still chained to the wall while the rats are on their way up the stairs from the basement, following the scent. What next? I still have no clue.

The phone rings. I pick up, grateful for the interruption.

"Tis me, old top," he says jovially.

Yes, tis my old friend Phineas Ogilvy, entertainment columnist for the *Los Angeles Times*, a closet heterosexual who is as well informed as he is flamboyant. Those who misread his sexual preference and underestimate his mental acuity do so at their own risk.

"Delighted to hear your voice, Phineas," I say.

"Yes, I get a lot of that. Once in a while it's even sincere. I hear you and Mirisch are about to sign Bob Wagner for Sam August."

"Working on it."

"Nice man. A good choice, old top. Certainly a better career move for Mr. Wagner than some insipid television series."

"What television series?" I ask.

"Not sure. Might be just a rumor. You know how this town is. So, tell me, Joseph, a source tells me that young Mr. Wagner was seen at the Valley police station the other day."

Uh-oh. Scandal alert.

"Was he? First I've heard of it. Probably dealing with parking tickets or some such."

"Thirty minutes with homicide sergeant Pedro Rodriguez? I doubt traffic had much to do with it. What can you tell me?"

Caught unawares I hesitate for the briefest of moments. Too late. My silence has given me away.

"What's going on, Joe? Surely you can share with me," Phineas says.

"I wish I could but I'm as surprised as you are, Phineas. You're positive about this?"

"Absolutely."

"I'm meeting with Bob later today. I'll ask him about it and get back to you. I'm sure it's nothing."

"Joe," Phineas says with a deep and sad inflection, "you wouldn't lie to an old friend, would you?"

"I'm insulted," I say in a huff.

"And I will be ready with an instant apology as soon as I see what you come back with."

"Look," I say, "it's been a long time between lunch dates. How about tomorrow?"

"An excellent suggestion. Come by my office at noon. Ta ta, dear friend. I shall count the minutes. Don't disappoint me."

Click. He hangs up. Immediately I dial up Cosmo Stryker.

"We are in deep trouble," I say when he comes on the line. I tell him about my conversation with Phineas and I can hear him muttering unintelligibly to himself on the other end of the line.

"Not to worry. I can deal with Phineas, Cosmo. I'll tell him the truth and he'll sit on it."

"You're sure?"

"I trust him with my life but Phineas isn't what worries me. He got tipped which begs the question, by whom was he tipped and who else knows what occurred? I know Bob asked me to back off but I don't think that is now possible. I suggest a sit down with you, me and the Wagners and the sooner the better."

"Bob isn't going to like this."

"I'm sure not but remind him when I was active in the biz, much of my responsibility was keeping names OUT of the papers. I still know how to do it."

"I'll get back to you," he says.

"Right away, Cosmo. No time to waste."

"Gotcha."

That evening right after dinner we convene a summit meeting at the Wagner home in Beverly Hills. Ray, Cosmo, the Wagners and me. I've already filled in Cosmo about King's dealings with a shylock. His people are going to ask around and maybe come up with a name. Wagner is still concerned that I am involved but not for the reason I supposed. He's learned of my near miss with heart failure last year and he wants me to be stress free. I tell Bob it's far more stressful knowing there's a killer out there who needs to be caught and caught quickly.

"Look, R.J." I say, "we have an unsolved murder on our hands and years back Marian was involved with the victim in a minor way. If the killer is caught and brought to justice, end of story. If he is not, the case will linger for months, maybe even years, but sooner or later, maybe as early as weeks from now, it will bust open and your names will surface. Cries of coverup and special privilege will ensue. The tabloids will plaster your faces all over their supermarket covers. I know the cliche. Any publicity is good publicity to which I say, cow manure. This kind of exposure you do not need. Ray? Cosmo?"

I look over at them and they nod in agreement.

"But you're okay?" Bob asks.

"I'm okay," I say, "and if I weren't I'd tell you so. Now tomorrow I'm having lunch with Phineas Ogilvy and I think between us we can divert the rest of the press from learning of Marian's dealings with the guy back when. But it isn't going to be enough. We are going to have to dig down, root out the man or maybe woman who committed this crime, and hand him or her over to Sergeant

Rodriguez on a spit. Are we agreed?"

I check their faces. We are agreed.

The following day I arrive at the *L.A. Times* building at eleven-fifty and walk into Phineas's office at twelve o'clock sharp. He is sitting at his desk reading that morning's *Daily Variety*. At a sideboard I spot six white cardboard food cartons with wire handles, a couple of plates and cutlery. Ah, Chinese. One of my favorites. I inhale deeply but the aroma of moo goo guy pan is not forthcoming. Instead I'm assaulted by an aroma akin to that of a dead polecat.

"What's the deal, Phineas? Usually we eat out," I say.

"Indeed we do, old top, but that was before last Monday when I stepped upon my scale and disabled it, the dial registering 306 pounds. I made the mistake of mentioning it to my physician, Doctor Misery—not his actual name, of course—whereupon he sat me down and described to me the consequences of my eating habits, the least of which was death. Included in his laundry list were inconveniences like constant pain in the extremities, difficulty walking, possible amputations, sexual impotence, forty minute bouts sitting on a toilet seat dealing with a rebellious digestive system, sleeplessness, chronic fatigue and finally a hospital bed from which I would not be permitted to rise. Reluctantly I put myself in his hands. The result is—" He points. "—that."

He hefts himself from his chair and moves to the sideboard where he starts to open the containers, one by one.

"Marinated brussel sprouts. Rutabaga rind. Boiled leeks. Shark skin sautéed in sea water. I forget what this one is but it's good,though. Tangy. And finally, shredded cactus spines boiled in coconut milk. A treasure trove of vitamins and minerals. In the past four days I have lost three and a half pounds."

He smiles at me. I smile back. He waves me over.

"Come join me," he says spooning some cactus spines onto his plate.

I grab a spoon and take a dab of everything. No more than one teaspoon of any one item. We sit down at his desk and I spell out my predicament while nibbling and forcing myself to go light on the rutabaga.

"The idea that either Bob or Marian could shoot someone is laughable," Phineas says. "Their involvement is coincidental and irrelevant."

"Of course but that won't prevent certain members of our journalistic brotherhood from making their lives a veritable hell if they pick up the scent."

"My thoughts exactly," Phineas says. "So, how may I help?"

"Bob has committed verbally to playing Sam August but contracts have yet to be signed. That much is true. I'd like you to devote tomorrow's column to the story, delving in detail as to how Bob is deep into procedural research in anticipation of bringing Sam to the screen. He is being mentored for the next week or so by LAPD homicide detective sergeant Pedro Rodriguez who is familiarizing him with the day to day life of a big city cop. Officers attached to the FBI and the Secret Service will also be participating in the near future. Their names have not yet been released. Blah, blah, blah. Can you handle it?"

Phineas smiles at me.

"Could Van Gogh paint irises? Could Gershwin compose symphonies? I shall compose a word picture of a man so devoted to the sanctity of his profession that no inconvenience nor imposition would prove too much."

"Lovely, Phineas, but I just need enough to rationalize Wagner's visit to the Van Nuys police station the other day."

"Cretin!" he explodes. "You come to me for help and I offer you truffles. You tell me you will settle for Tootsie Rolls."

"You're right," I say defensively. "What was I thinking? Handle it any way you wish, old friend, and we all will be most grateful."

"As well you should be," he harrumphs, downing a spoonful of leeks.

I feel good about Phineas. This isn't the first time he'll fudge his column for a good cause and it won't be the last. Because his column will be so lengthy and detailed about Bob Wagner's tutelage into police procedures no one will want to play second banana to the story so the press will leave it alone. Unless there is an unexpected development, the Wagners will be safe from scrutiny.

When it comes to law enforcement I have three sources of information and cooperation. Two of them- Aaron and Pete with the best of motives- have now frozen me out. That leaves Mick Clausen, the city's number one bail bondsman and the husband of my first wife Lydia. Happily there is no rancor among the three of us and whenever I show up at Mick's place of business near the courthouse, he is always happy to help out any way he can.

"No! Absolutely not! Are you nuts?"

This is a new and totally unexpected response from Mick whom I had found in his office checking payroll.

"I haven't even told you what I need," I protest.

"I don't care. You are not a well man, Joe, and yet you refuse to slow down and worse, you continue to stick your nose into police business where it does not belong."

"Wrong, Mick. If the police were smart enough to make what I need their business, I wouldn't be here bugging you."

"Good. Aaron and Pete care about you as much as I do."

"That's one way of looking at it. Erroneous, of course. Mind if I sit down?" Before he can reply, I do.

"You may have noticed, Joe, that I have a happy marriage and I intend to keep it that way. Not only have I been warned by Bunny to ignore your escapades in the world of criminal justice but Lydia has threatened me with banishment to the guest bedroom if I so much as ask you 'What's new?'"

"Come on, Mick, I am in no danger and I won't be. All I need is a name which I will immediately turn over to Pete Rodriguez. That is the entire extent of my participation. The least you could do is listen before you freeze me out."

He hesitates, then leans back in his chair eyeing me warily.

"I'll give you two minutes and then out you go."

I make the most of those two minutes and actually wind up my narrative with seven seconds to spare. By now Mick has leaned forward, elbows on his desk, listening intently.

"I can think of three loan sharks that might be involved but none of them would be stupid enough to commit murder, certainly not over twenty-five thousand dollars."

"My thoughts exactly, Mick," I say. "Cosmo, too. He's also checking around but reluctantly. I agree that murder doesn't make good business sense but what's left?"

A long pause.

"Robert Wagner," Mick says, drumming his fingers on his desk. "I've always liked him. He'd be good."

"I think so," I say.

More drumming on the desktop.

"Cosmo has his sources, I've got mine. I could have my boys ask around," he says.

"I'd appreciate it."

"Beneath the Twelve Mile Reef, it's one of Lydia's favorite movies."

"I remember."

"If she ever got a chance to meet Wagner, she'd probably faint."

"I could arrange it," I say.

He nods thoughtfully, mulling it over.

"If I came up with a name, you and me, we'd take it to Pete Rodriguez."

"Sure."

"Together."

"Absolutely."

"None of this you pasting on a phony mustache and wearing a wire and trying to get a confession from the guy in the back room of some cat house."

"Never crossed my mind."

Mick nods again, then says, "I'll see what I can do."

"Terrific!" I beam.

"No guarantees. We may come up empty."

"Understood."

"Okay. Now get out of here. Go home. Go to your office. Write your book."

Great idea. I consider asking Mick what he would do about Sam's predicament with the rats but decide he wouldn't have a clue any more than I do.

I leave his office and jog across the street to my car which is parked at curbside. Thunderclouds have started to gather and the sky is darkening. Rain is on the way. Time to get home to a warm dry house. A nattily dressed man is standing by my prized vintage Bentley, peering in through the driver side window. I tap him on the shoulder.

"Excuse me," I say.

He immediately steps aside.

"Sorry," he says. "Just admiring your ride. Used to have one just like it," he continues in a decidedly British accent. "She treat you well?"

"For the most part," I say, opening the car door and sliding in behind the steering wheel. As I pull my door shut, I am aware that the rear door is opening. I glance in my rear view mirror and see that the stranger has made himself at home. I see also that he is holding a nasty looking revolver.

"Just drive," he says politely. "I'll let you know where."

I fire up the engine still watching him.

"You aren't by any chance a loan shark?" I ask him.

"Nothing quite that despicable, Mr. Bernardi," he responds with a smile. "I'm a lawyer."

CHAPTER TWELVE

I pull away from the curb and when ordered, turn onto Hill Street. Almost immediately I find myself cruising through the heart of Chinatown with its red, green and gold silk dress shops, indecipherable ideograms, souvenir tourist traps and myriad restaurants. The smell of broiled pork and spicy chicken invades my senses even with my windows closed and I suddenly have a yen for Mongolian beef. I doubt it is shared by my passenger who suddenly presses the barrel of his gun against the back of my head.

"Up ahead, turn left onto Stadium Way," he says.

"What for? There's nothing there but the ballpark and the Dodgers are out of town," I say.

"I know. Drive."

I make the turn and head up the road toward the stadium parking area. Halfway up, my companion says, "Pull over." I do as I'm told.

"Why are we stopping?" I ask.

"Cut the engine."

Again I comply. For several moments we sit in silence.

"Okay," I say, "obviously this isn't a carjacking. What do you want?" I ask.

"Conversation," he says. "In private."

"You first."

"You've been bandying my name about with little regard for either my privacy or my good name and perhaps more important, the good name of my traveling companion."

"Who told you that?"

"Garrison King."

"Ah, then that would make you Dylan Pfieffer."

"It would indeed."

"A solicitor who abducts people at the point of a gun. Does the Crown know about this?"

"The gun is to make sure you did nothing stupid. You are in no danger, Mr. Bernardi. Here, I'll put it away."

I watch in the mirror as he slips the pistol into his jacket pocket.

"Could we get out of the car, Mr. Pfieffer? I'm getting a crick in my neck from having to look back at you."

"Certainly. Please exit first," he says.

I get out of the car, he follows suit leaving the pistol in his jacket pocket. He's not a big man, maybe five-eight, thin, pale with sad dachshund eyes. He looks me over, then reaches in his pocket and takes out a pack of Camels. He lights up and tosses the burnt match on to the ground as he walks over to a hip high wall and stares down at the city.

"I much prefer your American cigarettes to ours. You do something to them. Enhance the flavor perhaps. They are definitely preferable. Would you care for one?"

"Don't use 'em," I say. "Tell me about Marigold Toms. A lovely woman I've been told but I've yet to meet her."

"Lovely. Yes, she's that and so much more. Thoughtful, intelligent—"

"Disloyal, indiscriminate—"

"You are speaking, sir, of the woman I love," he flares. "We intend to marry this weekend at a chapel in Las Vegas."

"Callous. Unfeeling—"

"I am trying to hold my temper, Mr. Bernardi."

"Hold it all you like, Pfieffer. You move in with the mother, mooch off of her for a while, then head for the hills when she becomes terminally ill. At some point you start playing house with her daughter and then when Mama gasps her last, you run off to Mob City to get married to Lady Marigold. Not the behavior of an English gentleman and certainly not that of a loving daughter."

"First of all, I am more Irish than English and certainly not a gentleman. Secondly, you know nothing of the situation that existed back in Belfast. It was Marigold, not I, that committed Prunella into the care of that dreadful hospice and if a loving moment had ever passed between the two of them, I failed to observe it."

"Then I have misjudged you," I say.

"You have, sir."

"Marigold's the bitch and you're just a bystander."

His eyes turn cold. Instinctively he reaches for the jacket pocket into which he had stashed his pistol.

"Don't waste my time, Pfieffer. You're a liar, a con man, and an opportunist but you're not going to shoot me."

"You're right. That would be foolish," he says, "so instead I am going to give you some advice. Do not write the screenplay for 'The Enchanted Palazzo', stay away from Garrison King and do not meddle in my affairs. While I am personally not a man of violence, I know men who are."

"Shylocks."

"Who?"

"Private investors. Freelance financiers. Loan sharks. Goons with broken noses who have an outlandish view of prevailing interest rates."

Pfieffer shakes his head.

"I know nothing of such people," he says. "Now let's get back in the car and you can drive me to the nearest taxi rank."

"As you wish," I say.

"I do wish, Mr. Bernardi, and you will be well served if you remember my admonition. Stay away from Garrison King and stay out of my life or our next meeting will entail a great deal more than mere conversation."

I cock my head in his direction curiously.

"You know, Mr. Pfieffer, I don't react well to threats."

"Not a threat, merely a warning."

"Either way, I have a vested interest in Bob Wagner's well-being and I have no intention of backing away from Horatio Cummings' murder."

"Suit yourself," Pfieffer shrugs.

Several minutes later I drop Pfieffer off at a taxi stand. I pull away mulling my next move which should be to go home and mind my own business. That, however, would be the coward's way out. I have several options, none of them good. I settle on Cosmo on the theory that he is the least likely to run into Bunny at the local supermarket and inadvertently say something stupid to give me away.

I find him at his office chatting with Gunnar Larsen. They both look up when I walk through the door and Cosmo actually smiles.

"I've been trying to get a hold of you for an hour, Joe," Cosmo says. "When you get home there will be a message on your answering machine from an insurance agent named Dunphy. That's me. The alias was in case your wife was listening."

"You have news," I say.

"Tough Tony Trippi," Gunnar says, invoking the name of the city's most notorious and dangerous loan shark.

"You're kidding."

"Nope. He was fingered by a competitor. I called him to verify. He freely admitted lending Garrison King 25 Gs at the usual rates. Tony and I go all the way back to grammar school. His cousin Angie

"Nope. Go home, Joe. Leave this to me and my boys. We'll find something. Might just take a while."

The next morning I arise with the sun, retrieve the morning *Times* from the front porch and start to read Phineas' column at the breakfast table. Bridget is scurrying about, percolating coffee, poaching eggs, squeezing oranges, and lightly toasting some sourdough bread. There are times when my wife treats me like a hired hand but Bridget can always be counted on to pamper and coddle me. Bunny is lucky that Bridget isn't thirty years younger.

Phineas has done a masterful job. The old scoundrel has even managed to wring several appropriate quotes from the mouth of Pete Rodriguez who is going along with this charade for the sake of the Wagners and their kids. As soon as I finish eating I retreat to my room, coffee mug in hand, to call Phineas and thank him for a job well done. He accepts my lavish praise with his usual absence of humility.

"Incidentally, old top, I believe you once mentioned to me a woman named Marigold Toms."

"I might have," I reply.

"She phoned and said she enjoyed my column immensely and then asked me if I knew Robert Wagner. How she thought I could have gotten all those juicy quotes without knowing the man I will never know but she was dead serious. My first inkling that the daily crossword puzzle was way beyond her mental capabilities."

"I'm beginning to reach the same conclusion," I say.

"Miss Toms wanted me to put her in touch with Wagner. She needed to warn him that Wagner and his wife were in great danger from a man named Horatio Cummings. My God, Joe, doesn't the woman read a newspaper or watch the news on television?"

"Apparently not," I say.

"And then of all things she wants me to meet with her so she can explain. I politely refuse and hang up on her. If I am to have a groupie, I would prefer it not be her."

As he speaks an idea comes to me.

"Phineas, if she should call back, don't take her call."

"Aha, a muse has stirred you. Excellent."

"Maybe so but please do as I ask. Bob and Marian will be ever so grateful."

As soon as I hang up, I dial the Biltmore and ask for Dylan Pfieffer. If he answers I will hang up. I get lucky. The voice that picks up is female.

"Miss Toms?" I say.

"Speaking."

"This is Phineas Ogilvy and I want to apologize for being so abrupt when last you called." I have lowered my voice an octave and added a flowery lilt that is unmistakably Ogilvy. It isn't hard. Phineas is almost caricature of himself.

"No offense taken, I assure you," she says.

Except for the cockney, I am reminded of Judy Holliday in 'Born Yesterday'.

"You suggested we meet. An excellent idea. I would love to hear what you have to say about Mr. Wagner and his relationship with Mr. Cummings."

"Not with him, with her," Marigold says."And it ain't good, dearie, I can promise you that."

"Do you know where the Farmers Market is on Fairfax Avenue?"

"No."

"But a cab could take you there."

"Why would I want to do that?"

"Because, as you said, Mr. Cummings is a dangerous man and I don't think we should be seen together."

"Oh, right," she says.

"Do you have some sort of silk bandana?"

"Sure."

"What color?"

"I got a red, a blue and a checkerboard."

"Wear the red one around your neck."

"What for?"

"So I can recognize you."

"Oh, yeah."

"Shall we say an hour from now. Eleven o'clock?"

"Why not?"

"And let's keep this to ourselves. No sense telling the world."

"Right you are, ducky."

I hang up. This meeting holds such promise. Me and Marigold and without Pfieffer. I can't wait.

The Farmers Market is a Los Angeles landmark, born some thirty years ago and now a destination for tens of thousands of tourists who descend on the city each year much as the locusts had their way with Pharaoh some three thousand years ago. Fresh produce is for sale everywhere but in addition one can find dozens of food stalls featuring ethnic delights of every description. I park nearby and walk over to Mauricio's which affords a good view of the entrances on 3rd Street as well as Fairfax. Mauricio's is pasta heaven for those with a Mediterranean palate. It's one of my favorites. I hope Marigold will agree. I have no wish to lunch on corned beef and cabbage or boiled mutton.

I spot her easily when she exits her cab. Red bandana, a frumpy dress, her bleached blonde hair tied in a pony tail. She seems short, very short, despite the fact that she is wearing heels. When I greet her, introducing myself and taking her arm, I estimate her height at no more than five feet. I had gambled that she had no idea what Phineas looked like and it is now obvious, she does not. I lead her to a table for two and order a bottle of chianti and an antipasto to start. She seems a little bewildered by her surroundings and my attentiveness. As the minutes pass, I realize that for Marigold, bewilderment is a permanent condition.

"So," I say after we toast ourselves with wine," tell me more about this Horatio Cummings."

"A real Pat and Mick Hampton Wick, he is, and the world would be better off if he were brown bread."

She says it with such conviction I am tempted to believe her. The problem is, I have no idea what she's talking about.

CHAPTER THIRTEEN

Cockney rhyming slang was devised ages ago to allow grifters and thieves within earshot of Bow Bells to communicate among themselves without being understood by tourists and the Bobbies. It survives to this day as do their shopworn con games still perpetrated on a gullible public. Professing ignorance, I beg Marigold for a translation which she gladly provides. Horatio Cummings is a sick prick and we'd all be better off if he were dead. I nod sagely but do not mention the fact that Cummings unclaimed body has already been shipped off to Potters Field, a final resting place for paupers and indigents or those unclaimed by family or friends.

"That's why I came to Los Angeles," Marigold says. "When I realized where Horatio had gone, I knew it was two and eight for Mrs. W—trouble, I mean—because of the way he talked about her, especially when he was drinking. A real battlecruiser he was. I knew I couldn't let it be. Never be able to live with myself."

"So you hopped a plane, abandoning your mother—"

"Here! Where'd you get that? Me Mum was doing just fine in the hospice. The sisters saw to that."

"She'd had a stroke."

"And she was better. Much better."

"Then why'd she die?"

"Don't know. Maybe just her time. And how is it you know so much about my life. You been spying on me, Mr. Ogilvy?"

"Of course not. Why would I do that?" I ask. "So you arrive in L.A. and go looking for Robert Wagner."

"That's right. To warn him, him and the trouble and strife, I mean, his wife. Horatio was mean, deep down mean. He treated me Mum like Pony and Trap—Sorry, I mean, badly. Like crap. All he could think of or talk about was revenge for what she had done to him—"

"Or what he had done to himself."

"He didn't see it that way, mate. Like I said, he was a sick man."

"So he's here, you're here and then your mother dies but you don't return to Belfast for the funeral."

"I was going to but Dylan—that's my fella, Dylan—he says the sisters are handling everything and besides, now that I don't have to worry about Mum, he says why didn't we get married and I says to myself, why not? We've been waiting long enough. He says he'll arrange everything including the bridal suite at the Flamingo which is where we're going come Saturday."

"But your mother's death, that came as a shock to you, I mean, you thinking she was getting better and all. "

"Yeah, it did," she says and I can see little tears forming in the corner of her eyes. "Dylan checked on her by phone. That was when he flew to Belfast with business he had to attend to, the same day the coppers grabbed me in the terminal."

"He didn't go by to see her?"

"He was going to but he got hung up with this client, a real estate developer. But while he was in the city he called the hospice and the doc, she said Mum was looking and sounding really good. Top of the tree. Her and me, we'd had our hard days but the last year or two things were good between us."

"Did they tell you what the exact cause of death was?" I ask.

"Being in the hospice and all and in her condition, I think they guessed it was a heart attack."

"But there was no autopsy. Nothing like that."

"Wouldn't know nothin' about that."

I nod, then look at her. She is staring at me curiously.

"What am I doing here?" she asks. "Why are you asking me all these questions?"

"Marigold, I can't believe that Dylan didn't tell you."

"Tell me what?"

"Horatio Cummings is dead. He was shot to death several days ago and his body dumped in a deserted alley in the small hours of the morning."

Her eyes widen. She shakes her head.

"That can't be."

"I'm afraid it is and my name is not Ogilvy, it's Bernardi. Joseph Bernardi."

"Copper?"

"No."

"You think I offed him?"

"Did you?"

"Yeah, me and my little popgun." She shoves herself away from the table and stands. "Piss off, mister, and stay away from me."

I dig into my wallet and take out one of my old Bowles & Bernardi business cards. I hand it to her.

"Look, you're angry. I understand. But if you get to the point where you need some help or advice, all you have to do is call."

She stares at the card with ill-disguised contempt.

"Yeah, I'll be sure to do that," she says her voice dripping with sarcasm. "My life is finally turning into somethin' and I won't be lettin' you spoil it, you get me? Come near me again and I'll make sure you regret it."

And with that, she tosses the card away and bustles off in the direction of Fairfax Avenue, no doubt in search of a cab. With nothing better to do, I go home.

I am at a dead end with Marigold Toms, nowhere with Garrison King, and quickly earning the animosity of men I once called friends. I suppose they still are but I know that none of them wants to answer to Bunny should fate have something ugly in store for me. I am also at a dead end with Sam August and I dread having to sit in front of my typewriter, my brain inoperable, and my ass getting itchier and itchier the longer I sit doing nothing. Still, I must. Advice from my friend Truman Capote. No matter the price in skipped meals and lost sleep, never let a block get the best of you. Persevere at all costs.

I park in the driveway and enter the house through the kitchen door. As I close the door behind me, I suddenly feel dizzy. I can't keep my balance. I grab the kitchen counter to keep from falling. No, not another heart attack! I have things to do, people to help, loose ends that need tying off. I am vaguely aware of the sound of breaking cutlery and a loud crash as the toaster falls to the floor and then suddenly I stop reeling and am steady again. Bridget bursts into the room. "Mother of God," she wails. "Are you all right,sir?" "I think so," I say. "Would you look at it, sir," she says. "My good cups and saucers on the floor, broken into pieces and the toaster most likely broken as well." "What happened?" I ask.' "What happened? Why, the earth moved, sir."

"It was an earthquake?" "It was, sir, and a big one at that. Praise be, no one was hurt." Still unsteady on my feet, I stumble out of the kitchen to the staircase and holding tight to the bannister, make my way upstairs into my office. I'm grateful Bunny and Yvette were not here though I doubt they'd have been hurt. The quake was violent but short lived. Inevitably aftershocks will ensue. They should be lesser in magnitude. At least I hope so.

I settle down in front off my typewriter and stare at the offending page, still staring back at me. And then it comes to me. Dolt! What is shacked up with my cousin Leo. Tony knows I'm not going to rat him out to the cops."

"I don't suppose he mentioned Horatio Cummings," I say.

"The man's name never surfaced but I doubt Tony had anything to do with Cummings' death. He likes to work deadbeats over with a baseball bat or brass knucks but homicide's a chump's game and he knows it. Anyway I've been in his place in Brentwood. Six bedrooms, six baths. He's not going to risk the needle for a lousy twenty-five thousand. You gotta look someplace else, Joe."

"But not the Wagners," I say.

"No, not the Wagners. They put up a tough front but they're good people, scared to death, and they don't deserve this crap."

"Garrison King," I say flatly looking from one to the other.

"Not likely unless seven people are lying to protect him," Gunnar says. "I've already checked four of them. They all tell the same story. Poker until about two a.m. when the game broke up."

"King could have hired someone," I suggest.

"And paid them with what?" Cosmo says. "The guy was flat broke. Still is."

"Maybe the medical examiner got the TOD wrong. It's happened before," I say.

"And it'll happen again," Cosmo says, "but I wouldn't bet my pension on it."

"We both know these forensic guys are basically guessing. He says between midnight and two a.m. What if he'd guessed time of death between one and three? That would fit."

"Providing King left the game carrying a gun, drove to the Sportsman's, plugged him and then dumped him in the alley without attracting attention and so on and so forth. You really want to go down that road?"

Cosmo stares at me waiting for a response.

"You got anything better?" I ask.

do I use for a brain? Is 46 suddenly the beginning of the end? Next year at this time will I be able to write anything more complicated than a shopping list? My four typing fingers fall on the keyboard.

Straining every muscle in his body, August pulls and yanks at his chains. No use. They are securely affixed to the wall. From far off, he can hear the squealing of the basement rats as they scurry up the staircase, lured by a scent reminiscent of a bacon cheeseburger. August resumes his struggle. His situation is hopeless. In a matter of minutes he will be on the wrong end of a feeding frenzy, sharp little teeth will be shredding his skin. Suddenly he is slammed viciously backward against the wall. The room spins crazily. The sound of the rats increases in intensity and then just as suddenly starts to ebb as he hears the little buggers scatter away. A muffled rumbling sound reverberates.

The candled chandelier is swinging to and fro out of control. The room continues to shudder. The glass in a window shatters and falls to the floor. Certain that it is only a matter of seconds before the room collapses on top of him, August again strains at the chains that trap him but this time there is give. He looks up and behind him. The cement that once securely anchored his chains has started to crumble.

* * *

The phone at my side rings. I glare at it.

"Not now!" I scream to my four walls but it's useless. They are deaf. The phone rings again and then again and finally I reach over to answer it.

"This had better be good," I snarl into the mouthpiece.

"Better than good, Joe. We may have gotten a break." A man's voice.

"Who is this?" I demand.

"Gunnar. Gunnar Larsen."

Suddenly the room starts to shimmy.

"Hold on!" I shout into the phone. It lasts only seconds and then is gone. "Did you feel that?"

"Feel what?" Gunnar says.

Where is this guy calling from? Iowa?

"We have to meet, Joe. You, me and Bob Wagner."

"What about?"

"Not on the phone."

"Where?"

"The Temple in the Clouds."

"Never heard of it," I say.

"That's because the studio just built it for the picture. It's where Newman gets the crap kicked out of him by Strother Martin and his gang of coyotes. You got a pencil and paper? I'll give you directions."

A few minutes later I'm cruising Sunset Boulevard, heading toward the Beverly Hills Hotel which is where Topanga Canyon Boulevard intersects. I turn and head north on this iconic twisty turning road, the scene of hundreds of car chases in Saturday afternoon serials like Spysmasher and Secret Agent X-9. My eyes search for an obscure turnoff which will lead to the summit of the mountains where Warners has erected a quirky prayer temple for an equally quirky cult which, it turns out, is a cover for a people-smuggling organization. A few moments later I break into the clear and there it is before me, a sort of faux-Greco edifice, complete with faux-Corinthian columns. Except for one car, the place looks deserted. I pull up a short distance from the other car and get out. As I do, two men exit the other car. One is Gunnar Larsen. The other man I do not recognize. He's tall and beefy, garbed in a five hundred dollar suit, a diamond stick-pin securing his Countess Mara tie. He has the face of a heavyweight who lost too many fights. They approach.

"No trouble finding the place?" Gunnar asks.

"None," I reply. "Where's Bob Wagner?"

"Not coming," Gunnar says. He indicates his companion. "Joe, this is Anthony Trippi. Tony, Joe Bernardi."

So here I am, face to face with Tough Tony Trippi, feared loan shark, and my trusty .25 caliber Beretta is in the glove box and I am wondering what sort of weenie roast I have been invited to. Gunnar must have sensed my apprehension. He smiles.

"No need to worry, Joe. We're all playing for the same team."

Trippi smiles and juts out his hand.

"Nice to meet you," he says.

We shake. When I get my hand back, I resist the temptation to count my fingers.

"I mentioned Wagner to make sure you showed, Joe. Tony has some information that might prove useful and I wanted you to hear it directly from him."

I nod.

"Here I am," I say.

"First thing, Joe. I didn't kill the guy. Not my style. I'd take a three to five for racketeering before I'd risk the needle on a murder rap. Anybody who kills is plain stupid and deserves what happens to them."

"Okay," I say.

"But that doesn't stop some people from trying to buy me."

"Garrison King."

"The kraut. That's right," Trippi says. "I went after him because twice he'd tried to stiff me on the vig and I told him there wouldn't be a third time. I told him to be sure his hospitalization insurance was paid up. He said he didn't have the money, this guy Cummings had the 25Gs and if I wanted it, that's where I'd find it. I told him I didn't do business with third parties. The kraut borrowed the money, the debt is his responsibility."

"Makes sense to me," I say.

"Then he tells me how this guy Cummings has him all fucked up and he would be better off if Cummings were dead and if I could arrange it, he would be grateful and make it worth my while. I say to him, how are you going to do that? You got no dough and no way to get any which is when he offers me points in the movie."

"Really?" I say, suddenly interested. "How many?"

"Two. I say to him, is that net, gross or modified gross? He says net. I tell him I wouldn't get out of bed for net. I do a lot of business with Hollywood types and I learn fast. So he changes his story and offers two points gross after deducting profit participation for the brain-dead babe who is in for adjusted net and is obviously in need of a new agent. King says the picture will bring in millions and I will become very rich. I tell him I am already very rich and he can take his points and stick 'em where the sun don't shine."

"And then he says what?"

"He whines and offers me three points. I tell him I will be back in three days and if he doesn't have my money, I will send him to Mt. Sinai in a coma. Of course, I do not actually mean this."

"Of course not," I echo. "And then some time in the next three days, Cummings ends up in an alley with two slugs in him," I surmise.

"He does," Trippi says. "So at the end of the third day I return to King's offices and tell him what a lucky guy he is, this jerk of a writer having been offed by person or persons unknown. He agrees with me that he is very lucky which is when I ask him for the vig. He says he doesn't have it but now he can get a script and raise money and make the movie and again he offers me the three points gross if I will show a little patience. At first I am averse to doing this but then I figure I have a shot at a big number and all I have to do is nothing and eventually, if my points are no good, I can still take it out of this Nazi bastard's hide."

"So you think what, Tony? That King did the job himself?"

"Why not? He had to do something and he had to do it quick. I say, yeah, I think he did it."

"He's got an alibi,"I say.

Trippi laughs out loud.

"I should damned well hope so," he says. "Who's got him covered? People who work for him? Actors or writers looking for a job? Bums who would, for a price, swear that JFK was killed by Hugh Hefner?" He shakes his head in mock amusement. "What's the sense of being a kraut if you can't kill people. It's a lesson I learned at Omaha Beach."

"You were part of the D-Day landing?" I say, more than a little surprised.

"Yeah. Me and a few thousand other guys."

"And you are coming forth with this now for what reason, Tony?" I ask.

"He's a fan," Gunnar says, "Of Mr. Wagner. When he heard Mr. Wagner was getting screwed over, he told me he wanted to help."

Tony nods.

"A few years back I saw the guy in that movie about the Titanic. Good movie and I liked the guy, how he was saving people and all and didn't die in the end. So what I knew I told Gunnar and Gunnar says I gotta tell you and that's it."

"That's it?"

"And also D-Day. Made me feel kind of proud. I was fighting for the American way of life, liberty and free enterprise, the right to conduct one's business without interference from the government. I believed it then. I believe it now. Especially that last part. Anyway, Bernardi, the short price is on the kraut. Do with it what you will."

CHAPTER FOURTEEN

Now I am up against it. It's just past six o'clock. I should be home getting ready for dinner with Bunny and the kid. I should also be in Pete Rodriguez's office feeding him the details of my meeting with Tough Tony Trippi. But a meeting with Pete or Aaron is incendiary because it may bring a caring but wrathful Bunny into the picture and this I do not need. I believe Trippi is right. Garrison King solved his problem the only way he knew how. Two pops from a pistol and his troubles were over. It's so simple and so obvious I have trouble believing it. But proof? Don't have any. No, if I am going to meet with Pete and Aaron I had better have something concrete to give them, not just the opinion of a notorious loan shark. If it weren't for that damned alibi, I think—and then it comes to me. I remember that it is Wednesday and unless I have been misled, a weekly poker game should be getting under way some time soon.

I have her name—Rosalie Birnbaum—and I know she lives in Reseda and by now she should be home. I go in search of a phone booth and a directory and moments later I am dialing her number.

"Yeah?"

It's her. I recognize the nasal inflection.

"Rosalie, it's Joe Bernardi. Remember me?"

"From the roller rink?" she asks hopefully

"No, the office. The new writer. Tall, good looking—"

"Oh, yeah, the old guy," she says with little enthusiasm.

"I have some pages I need to get to Mr. King right away. Could you give me his home address, please."

"I'm not supposed to do that, "she says and I hear a tiny little pop. She's chewing gum.

"I understand but he's told me it is hugely important he receive this material early this evening and if he doesn't get it, he says heads will roll. I assume he means me and anyone else who stands in his way and frankly, I need this job. Not a good time to be out of work."

Silence and then the light dawns and she supplies me the address for a high rise in Brentwood. She even gives me the unit number. Good. If the building has underground parking, this will allow me to bypass lobby security. I hustle over there, park on the street and walk down the ramp into the garage for occupants only. I call the elevator and punch the button for the third floor. In a few moments I'm leaning on the bell for 3C.

A mousy little man wearing rimless spectacles answers the door. For a moment I think I recognize him but I'm not sure.

"Yes?" he says.

"Here to see Garrison King," I say displaying my warmest smile.

The little fella hesitates, then shouts inside.

"Garry? You expecting anybody?"

"No!" comes King's voice.

"Probably forgot all about me," I say pushing past him and into the condo's spacious living room. Five men are standing around, drinks in hand. One of them is Garrison King. When he sees me, he smiles and waves me forward.

"Mr. Bernardi, this is a pleasant surprise. Come in, please."

"Sorry to intrude," I say, "but I remember you telling me that Wednesday was poker night and since it's a game I love I thought

I'd drop by on the chance you might have an open seat."

"*Ach*, I am sorry," he says, "but we play seven handed, no more, and we are waiting for the arrival of our seventh so we can begin. But may I offer you a drink?"

"No, no. I'm really sorry. It was stupid of me to show up like this."

My eyes scan the others. They are middle aged, well dressed and professional looking. I was expecting lowlifes who would rat out their mothers for a hit on a bong. It seems I am mistaken and may be running a fool's errand here.

"Have a drink, Bernardi," one of the others says. "We're waiting for Butch, totally unreliable, lives in a world of his own. For all we know he's flying his Piper Cub to Vegas for a fling at the crap tables."

"Well, in that case," I say with a smile.

For the next fifteen minutes I nurse a beer while chatting with the others and awaiting the arrival of Preston "Butch" Kerwin, a borderline successful real estate broker specializing in bank repos. The tall fellow in the herringbone sports jacket is an artists manager who reps at least a dozen Grammy winners. The little guy at the door has had his picture in the paper a lot lately. He is an ambulance chasing attorney representing a battered wife on a murder charge. One player owns a boutique hotel on the Sunset Strip while another is a police lieutenant attached to the Hollenbeck Division. I assume there's a minimal chance we will be raided by the cops this evening.

After twenty minutes it becomes painfully obvious that Butch is not going to show and the conversation turns in his direction.

"I think we've lost him for good," Herringbone says. "The lucky bastard."

"I say no loss," the lawyer chimes in. "I was getting real tired of his whining every time he lost a couple of hundred bucks. Now that he's got seven million to toss away, we can look around for a new face. Maybe yours, Mr. Bernardi," he says with a smile.

"Maybe so," I reply, "but what's with this seven million dollars?"

"Butch's old man. Forty eight years old, in great health and pow, he chokes to death on a dim sum in a Chinese restaurant. He was a widower, Butch was an only child. Go figure."

"God is good," Herringbone says.

"God is misguided," the lawyer corrects him.

A few minutes later, the game starts and I am in a prized seat. The buy-in is five hundred dollars. Since I don't walk around with that kind of money, Garrison King vouches for me. After an hour I have lost the five hundred and an hour after that I have lost five hundred more. It's not that I'm a lousy poker player- I'm not- but my mind is not on the game, it is elsewhere. When I lose a second rebuy I apologize and take my leave as six avid poker players pray fervently that I will return the following week. I have left behind a check for $1500 and I haven't whined. To these guys, Joe Bernardi is a marked improvement over Butch Kerwin.

I get in my car and start back toward home, my brain clicking like an adding machine as little bits and pieces come together to form a mosaic. I remember that in Marigold's correspondence which I came across in Horatio's motel room, mention was made of reciprocal wills between Horatio and Prunella Toms, Marigold's mother. Probably meaningless at the time. Prunella had to be committed to a charitable hospice and Horatio's books weren't selling worth a damn. But that was then and this is now and the matter of a $175,000 contract has entered the picture. Numbers like that turn an estate into an Estate and now I put my brain to work dredging up a little of what I know of the law which is, sadly, very little.

Basically, Prunella inherits from Horatio, Horatio inherits from Prunella and that's as complicated as it gets but as I recall, there's more to it than that. Survival enters into the equation. Okay, Horatio Cummings is shot to death and at that moment Prunella, still alive, inherits all of Horatio's worldly goods including that $175,000 contract for the rights to 'The Enchanted Palazzo'". Granted, $175,000 is not millions. Neither is it a bag of candy corn. So for a short period of days, Prunella is quite well off. And then, tragically, her life is snuffed out by causes unknown and presumably her now considerable estate devolves to her daughter Marigold, the same Marigold Toms who is on the verge of running off to Vegas to marry Dylan Pfieffer. This is the same Dylan Pfieffer who was in Belfast at or very near to the time of death for Prunella. He denies having dropped in to see her and now here he is about to marry into a great deal of money which, I suspect, his bride to be knows nothing about.

Murder most foul? Possible? Yes. Plausible? Not sure but it fits a lot better than anything else I can come up with. I know, too, that I have got to share this with someone and that someone is Pete Rodriguez except that Pete is a zealot where my well-being is concerned and he may ignore what I have to say in favor of carping about my self-destructive behavior. Aaron, on the other hand— Yes, much better. Aaron is older and mellower and we go back a long way. Almost twenty years. Aaron won't like what I've been doing but he'll listen.

I pull into the driveway and park by the kitchen door. When I walk inside, I find Bunny in p.j.s and bathrobe sitting at the kitchen table glaring at me.

"What?" I say defensively. "I told Bridget I wouldn't be home for supper, that I'd be late."

"You've been out or late almost every night this week, Joe. We've got a little girl upstairs who asked me tonight if you were going to go live somewhere else. Apparently divorce runs rampant among the parents at her school and very honestly she is scared to death."

"Oh, God," I say. "Bunny, I am so sorry. I'll go up and talk to her."

"No, you won't, Joe. She's asleep. When you didn't come home, she went to bed early."

I flop down on one of the kitchen chairs, shaking my head. I don't get flummoxed easily. This is one of those times.

"Where were you, Joe, and don't tell me you were working because we both know that would be a lie."

"No, not working. I was—" Oh, God, this is going to sound awful. "I was playing poker."

"Poker," she says flatly.

"Poker. I went to King's condo because I had to clear up a couple of things on my contract and there were a bunch of guys there about to sit down for a game and one of the regular guys didn't show and I got talked into sitting in."

"And how did you do?" she asks, obviously disbelieving.

"I won about six hundred bucks," I lie. I am not about to be a shithead and a loser in the same breath.

"Great," she says holding out her open hand. "I'm going to need a new dress for Gloria's birthday party next Friday."

"Sorry, kiddo. All I've got is IOUs but tomorrow you're going to take a long lunch hour, I'm going to drive you to Rodeo Drive where you can pick out your frock at some outrageously overpriced boutique and then we'll have lunch at Scandia. Deal?"

I get up and walk over to her, lean in and give her a big smack on the lips. She shakes her head, trying her best to stifle a laugh.

"Damn you, Joe Bernardi, you are such a con man," she giggles whereupon I kiss her again, much more seriously this time and she responds in kind. Can the bedroom be far behind? Chalk one up for the con man.

At nine-fifteen in the morning Aaron is invariably his usual irascible self and today is no different. He's at his desk poring over reports that chronicle the extent of homicide in Los Angeles. Homicide is his beat, always has been, and now that he is the big cheese in the department, I think he's had enough of it. At age 50 he has three more years before his pension will be totally vested and I'm pretty sure he's counting the days.

"I love you, Joe, I really do," he says, "and you are not only a terrific writer but a terrific friend as well. But this—this mish-mosh—you haven't brought me a murder, you've brought me an episode of 'Dragnet'. No, maybe not that realistic."

"Aaron, open your brain cells, Let the sun shine in. Pete's got a case that is growing colder by the hour and will have grown to a glacier by the weekend. Okay, I have a theory but it's a good one and it could turn out to be correct. What the hell are you so afraid of that you won't listen?"

Aaron leans back in his chair.

"Okay," he says. "Give it to me again. Slowly. From the top."

I repeat myself and this time I think he's actually listening instead of musing about how he will toss me out of his office with a minimum amount of fuss. When I finish, I add, "All it takes is one phone call to Belfast, Aaron. Was there or was there not an autopsy and if not, why not?"

He stares at me, mulling it over, and then presses his intercom button.

"Sir," comes the voice of his aide.

"Belfast, Northern Ireland, Sergeant. Connect me with the police. I need to speak to their Inspector General or whoever the hell's the man in charge."

"Yes, sir."

Aaron looks over at me.

"You know, Joe, I'm pretty sure you're not insane—"

"Thanks for that," I say.

"—but I'm not sure you don't have a death wish. Your health is suspect and yet you keep running around, poking your nose where it doesn't belong, often begging people to pop you one and what for? Ego? Something you need to prove, if not to others, then to yourself. You have a beautiful and loving wife, a terrific kid, you're richer than Getty and yet, none of it is enough. What the hell is your problem?"

"I don't know," I say,

"Oh, bullshit," Aaron growls.

"No, I mean it, Aaron. I'd be perfectly happy to be left alone with my books and my family but every time I turn around, I'm getting sucked into something. I need Bob Wagner for my movie but Bob's in deep trouble—"

"And so you consider it your personal responsibility to solve his problem for him. Right? Like digging your buddy Army McLeod out of that pickle in the Arizona desert or covering for Orson Welles in the death of that slick porno movie producer. You know who you are, Joe? You're the old woman in the shoe with all those kids to take care of and you can't leave it alone. Anybody with a sad story or a load of misery, you're right there. You shoulda been a social worker, or maybe even a priest.

"Come on, Aaron—"'

"No, you come on, Joe. You may be the luckiest guy I know and you put it all at risk every morning when you get up. I don't know who killed this writer but I do know that if you keep poking around with a stick, you could end up the same way."

"Are you finished?"

"For now," Aaron says.

Bzzz. Aaron punches the intercom button.

"Yes?"

"His name's Seamus Ryan, Chief Superintendent with the Police Service of Northern Ireland."

"Right," Aaron says, picking up the phone and activating the speaker so I can listen in. Ryan has a deep authoritative voice, a brogue as thick as black molasses and he's all business. To the best of his knowledge no autopsy was performed on Prunella Toms. The staff physician at the hospice signed the death certificate listing cause of death as natural causes. No, this was not unusual. Dozens of

148

elderly and ailing people are cared for at the Christ, the Redeemer hospice and a death a week, sometimes two, is not unusual. The hospice is run by the Episcopal Church and has a spotless reputation.

A few moments later, Aaron hangs up and looks over at me.

"Satisfied?" he asks.

"I suppose," I say.

But I'm not.

CHAPTER FIFTEEN

No, I am not satisfied, not at all. For all the four star ratings lavished on Christ the Redeemer by the local gendarme-in-chief, one fact remains. No autopsy was performed on Prunella Toms and as long as that is the case, my suspicions linger. The problem is, I don't know what to do about them. Short of hopping a plane to Belfast, I am helpless to dig deeper and even if I were inclined to fly to Northern Ireland, I'm not sure how I would be able to do it under Bunny's cute but curious nose. Less satisfactory would be investigating by phone but that, too, would require some fancy footwork. To reach people during Belfast working hours I would have to telephone in the dead of night, Los Angeles time. How exactly would I slip out of bed at one in the morning without arousing Bunny's suspicions, and if I tell her nature is calling —I have a bothersome prostate—she may begin to worry when twenty or thirty minutes pass and I still gave not returned to bed. She may come looking for me and, finding me sitting at my desk and not on the throne, she might suspect I was up to something. No, I am at an impasse with no solution in sight.

And then fate intervenes. Bunny casually mentions that her boss, Jim Kelso, will be out of town for two days starting the day after tomorrow. The NNEA (National Newspaper Editors Association) is gathering in Oklahoma City and while Jim hates the phony camaraderie and time wasting revelry which accompanies the event, he considers it his obligation to attend and represent the newspaper. Aha!

I call him from my office the first thing the following morning, even before Bunny is out of the shower and putting herself together presentably as women are wont to do. I beg him to send Bunny in his stead and learn that he would be delighted except that he felt he would be selfish in doing so, Bunny being married and having a husband and a child to care for. I tell him to feel as selfish as he wants and that I will be entirely in his debt. If he wonders why, he is too much of a gentleman to ask.

The next day I see Bunny off on a noon flight to Oklahoma after which I drive straight to the Brickhouse building which houses the offices of Bowles & Bernardi, the management firm that still bears my name and which continues to pay me a modest monthly stipend for my occasional contribution when needed. When I walk through the double doors into the reception area, I get a lot of smiles and handshakes. Gretchen, our gorgeous Austrian receptionist who had once made it her life's work to snare me when I was available, gives me a hug and kiss. She is now happily married with a year old daughter and I am old news. I drop by Bertha's office. More hugging and kissing. Bertha Bowles is one of the three most powerful women in the Hollywood firmament. Years ago she persuaded me to join her in a partnership that eventually made us both wealthy beyond our dreams. I opted for a change in careers, she didn't, and she is still at it, happily turning talented newcomers into industry icons. There's no one like her. Finally I make a beeline for the office of Glenda Mae Brown, my gorgeous ex-secretary, ex-Gal Friday and at one time, an indispensable part of my career. I love her, always have, and always will. These days she is a talented publicist, the brightest in our lineup of very bright staffers. More hugging but not so much kissing. Our relationship never went beyond deep friendship, affection and respect. She was married and I was not about to lose a much-valued career partner for a quick and transitory roll in the hay. On that I think we both agreed.

"What are you doing here, boss? Slumming? And where the hell is your Pulitzer Prize?" she wants to know.

"Working on it," I say. "So, gorgeous, what are your plans for tonight?"

"Same old, same old," she says. "Hamburger helper and low fat ice cream followed by Beau and me curled up on the sofa watching Bob Hope and Danny Kaye."

"I didn't mean this evening, I meant tonight. After midnight."

"Why you dirty old man," she laughs.

"Tell Beau to get along without you. I need you."

"He'll be thrilled to hear it."

I explain. I have to place an important call to Belfast around two a.m. I can't do it from home because the call will appear on the phone bill and Bunny, my wife, keeper, and unofficial head nurse, has all of my activities under constant surveillance. I also need Glenda Mae's stenographic skills. If I'm lucky I'm going to be acquiring a lot of much needed information.

"What makes you think that I am not a part of the surveillance squad?" she asks me.

"Oh, God, no," I say.

"Oh, God, yes," she replies. "The list includes everyone you know including the parking valet at Chasen's."

I sag into a chair by her desk, defeated. She looks down at me with compassion in her eyes.

"What is it this time?" she asks. "Another helpless mope who can't get along without the Bernardi lifeline?"

I shake my head and tell her. She listens intently, then says, "I love Sam August and Robert Wagner would be perfect."

"Yes, he would."

"But if Bunny finds out I'm helping you she'll never forgive me."

"Well, she's not going to find out from me. For God's sakes, Glenda Mae, it's a lousy phone call, not the Boston Marathon and I am feeling great. Never better."

I must have made a pitiful sight because she relented and that night at quarter to two we find ourselves in her office. She's put on a pot of her chickory-laced coffee and brought in crullers. She's also gotten the phone number for Christ the Redeemer hospice in Belfast where it is quarter to ten in the morning.

As I sip my coffee, she punches the speaker button and then dials the number. A few moments later, the call is answered by a female with a lilting brogue.

"Christ the Redeemer, this is Mona. How may I help you?"

"Good morning, Mona. My name is Joseph Bernardi, I am fairly well known American author researching a book and if possible I would like to speak to your staff physician if he is available."

"That would be a she, sir. Dr. Tierney. I'll buzz her office and see if she is available. Please hold."

I look over at Glenda Mae and nod with a smile. So far, so good. After a few moments another female voice comes on line.

"This is Karen Tierney," she says, "I'm sorry, Mona didn't catch your name."

"Joseph Bernardi, Doctor. I'm an American novelist doing some research for a new book and I am hoping you might be able to help me."

A momentary silence.

"What was that name again?" she asks.

"Joseph Bernardi."

More silence.

"A Family of Strangers? That Joseph Bernardi?" she asks,

My first novel and she's actually read it. I can't believe it.

"Yes, that's me," I say.

"I loved your book, Mr. Bernardi. Truly I did."

I'm thrilled beyond words.

"Thank you so much," I say.

"I also saw the movie. The screenwriter should be drawn and quartered."

"Really?" is all I can manage to mutter. Dr. Tierney obviously pays no attention to screen credits. The screenwriter was me.

"Well, perhaps the scenarist was a little heavy handed," I say.

"No matter. The book's the thing. It will survive long after that film has run its course on ITV's graveyard hours. Now Mr. Bernardi, how is it I may help you?"

"Well," I say, warming up my bullshit machine, "I'm working on a new book which is set in Northern Ireland—lots of action and intrigue due to the troubles."

"I can imagine," she says.

"For better or for worse I do not take sides but I have a major character who has fallen seriously ill and is confined to a hospice for round the clock care. I need to kill her off without raising suspicion that her demise was anything other than natural causes and I am hoping you can advise me how to handle that."

"Well, I'm sorry, Mr. Bernardi, but you are the writer, not me. In any case it would be almost impossible."

"Oh, you mean the autopsy."

"No. If the person were very sick, no autopsy would be required but the doctor filling out the death certificate would easily spot many things that might arouse suspicion."

"Such as?"

"Bruising, ligature marks, needle tracks, burst blood vessels in the eyes in the event of suffocation. Those are the obvious ones. There are others known to a qualified physician."

"And if this qualified physician happened to run across one or more of these markers, he or she would order an autopsy to be performed."

"Absolutely."

I look over at Glenda Mae who is furiously taking everything down on her steno pad. I throw her a smile. She smiles back.

"Could you give me an example, Doctor? One of these obscure methods of inflicting death?"

"I'd rather not," she says. "Some loon might use your book for research and I would be a long distance accessory. No, thanks."

"Let's say I didn't actually put it in the book, just stored it away under useful trivia."

"Well, if you're not going to put it in your book, then why are you calling me?" There's a momentary silence. "There is no book, is there, Mr. Bernardi?"

"Actually, no," I say.

"Then what's this all about?"

"Prunella Toms."

Another silence ensues and then she says, "Tell me."

And so I tell her in great detail about the possibilities and my suspicions.

"What you are suggesting is monstrous, Mr. Bernardi," she says when I am finished. "You are accusing one of my people of murder."

"No, ma'am, I am not but I am wondering if Mrs. Toms might have had a visitor on the day that she died."

"I don't know. Please hold."

I hear her giving muffled instructions while she has covered the mouthpiece of the phone and a moment later she is back with me.

"Sister Agnes is the head nurse on that floor. I've summoned her. This make take a few minutes."

We sit mostly in silence for the next few minutes. She says more nice things about my book, I ask her about the hospice which has been around for decades, catering to the underprivileged regardless of religion. And then she excuses herself and re-covers the mouthpiece. This goes on for over a minute and then she is back.

"Sister Agnes says that Mrs. Toms had one visitor on that day, Mr. Pfieffer, her solicitor and a good friend of Mrs. Toms daughter, Marigold."

"And can she remember the time gap between his departure and Mrs. Tom's time of death?"

More phone covering, more mumbling.

"Twenty minutes to half an hour as best she can recall," Dr. Tierney says.

"Was Mrs. Toms on any sort of intravenous drip?" I ask.

"Yes, a mild morphine solution for her pain."

"And suppose that Mr. Pfieffer was able, unobserved, to introduce an air bubble into the drip line, how long do you suppose before that would kill her?"

The doctor pauses.

"For a layman, you seem to know a lot about murder, Mr. Bernardi," she says.

"That's not an answer to my question, Doctor."

"Then let's say no more than an hour, probably a lot less."

"Thank you, Doctor, you've been a great help."

"Several of those other methods I alluded to would also fit your scenario, Mr. Bernardi."

"And thank you again."

"If something develops on your end, I'd appreciate a call," she says.

"You'll be at the top of my list," I tell her and after another heartfelt thank you, I hang up. I look over at Glenda Mae.

"Pretty flimsy, boss," she says.

"Hardly an eyewitness account but he killed her, Glenda Mae. Bet the family jewels on it."

"And you are sure of this because—?"

"Because Pfieffer told the woman's daughter that while in Belfast he conducted only business, never went near the hospice and never saw Prunella."

"Damning but hardly evidence. It won't hold up," she says.

"Of course it won't which is why I have to approach this from a totally different angle."

I knew going in that I wouldn't dig up definitive proof and so I had devised a secondary plan of action which I put into effect the following day by contacting Cosmo Stryker. Logically I should have brought my plan to either Aaron or Pete but that would have gained me nothing except a set of handcuffs and an indeterminate time in a jail cell. At that moment Bunny would be required to bail me out and after that—well, I don't even want to contemplate 'after that'.

Cosmo listens attentively to what I have in mind and, while he doesn't say so, I believe he thinks my idea is an inch or two short of lunacy. Nonetheless he agrees to cooperate. Step one.

Step two requires a phone call to Pfieffer at the Biltmore. It's nearing noon when he answers the phone. He recognizes my voice immediately and I get the sense he is not happy to hear from me.

"It's too late for lunch but how about dinner, you and me, at the Brown Derby this evening? My treat," I say.

"No, thanks."

"We have business to discuss," I say.

"I doubt that."

"Okay," I say with an audible sigh. "Then I guess I'd better go straight to Sergeant Rodriguez. I wanted to discuss this with you first as a matter of courtesy, but if you're not interested, I apologize for bothering you. I suspect you'll be hearing from the sergeant later today."

I hesitate for just a moment before hanging up which is when he says "Wait!" into the phone. "What time this evening?" he asks.

"Seven-thirty," I say. "I'll make the reservation."

"I'll be there," Pfieffer says and then hangs up.

I move on to step three which involves my old pal Tildy Thayer, now working behind the reservations desk at the Sportsman's Lodge. When she hears what I have in mind she quickly agrees to participate. While it's an acting job of sorts, it isn't much of a part. Nonetheless she is intrigued.

The trap is baited. Now all that remains is for the rat to get a whiff of the cheese.

CHAPTER SIXTEEN

Los Angeles is an idiosyncratic city and among the bizarre things in which it takes pride is it's nonconforming restaurants. The most famous may be a cafe shaped like a hot dog on a bun. A close second would be the Brown Derby which is the name of several sites, the most famous of which is located on Wilshire Boulevard. Yes, it was built in the shape of a brown derby, the kind worn by Popeye's pal, Wimpy. Because of the allusions to it made by so many radio comedians it is a mecca for tourists and always busy. A few celebrities still show up, those who need to be seen and talked about to further their careers. The more secure mostly dine elsewhere.

Carmine, the maitre'd has shown me to a comfortable booth that looks out over the boulevard and I order a cold Coors while I wait for my dinner companion. My watch reads seven-thirty-one when he steps through the door. I wave to him and he heads toward me on a beeline, bypassing Carmine who is attending to another couple.

"This had better be good, Bernardi," he says abruptly as he slides into the booth opposite me. "I've got a lot on my plate and no time for bullshit."

"I wouldn't dream of wasting your valuable time, Mr. Pfieffer, but we are both anxious to see Mr. King's film made and I believe we would do just about anything to see it come to fruition. Short of murder, of course, but in that regard, I speak only for myself."

Our waiter draws near. Pfieffer waves him away in annoyance as I continue.

"I have a substantial writing fee riding on this film not to mention five—count 'em—five points of net profits when it's released. Frankly, I need the money and nobody is going to jeopardize that. Especially you, Mr. Pfeiffer."

"I still don't know what you're talking about," he growls.

"I'm talking about murder. I'm talking about you taking down Horatio Cummings by putting two slugs in him and then dumping him in a dark deserted alley so King could get a script and start filming. I'm talking about greed, a character trait we share in abundance."

"You're crazy!" he says.

"I don't think so," I reply. "You desperately wanted this deal to go through so you took matters into your own hands without giving a second thought to the others involved in this production, me being one, Garrison King being another and last but not least, Anthony Trippi.

"Who?"

"Tough Tony Trippi, a shylock who handed 25 grand to King and now is threatening to tear his throat out. When that happens, goodbye picture and you and I are out in the cold, not to mention your girlfriend who inherits that $175,000 contract for the rights to the book, a contract which has suddenly become worthless."

He shrugs.

"King may have screwed up but as for me killing somebody, you're daft."

"You were seen."

"What?"

"In the alley. That night. The night Cummings was killed. There was a witness."

"You're off your nut," he says.

"Am I?"

I look past his shoulder and nod. He turns to see what I am looking at. Cosmo and Tildy are standing together by the reservation desk. She's looking at Pfieffer, then turns to Cosmo and whispers confidentially in his ear. He listens, nods, then gives me one final look and the two of them quickly exit the premises. Tildy Thayer, even though no longer young, is a striking looking woman and I am counting on the fact that Pfieffer will remember seeing her at the Sportsman's Lodge. He does not disappoint. He turns back to me and I can see ill-disguised fear in his eyes.

"Who was that?" he asks.

"Who was what?" I ask innocently.

"The woman at the desk."

"What woman?"

"Standing next to the man. At the desk."

"I don't know who you're talking about."

"You must have seen them. They were looking right at you."

"You're seeing things."

He squirms in his seat, takes another look back, then takes a long swallow from his water glass. He looks at me, his eyes registering panic. Sweat is starting to form at his hairline.

"I won't be blackmailed," he whines.

"Who said anything about blackmail?" I ask. "Look, Pfieffer, you killed Cummings. You know it and I know it. Maybe it was a good thing. Maybe now we all get our money but I'll tell you one thing and I will only tell you only once. Another stunt like the one you pulled up by Dodger Stadium and I go to the police and you go to San Quentin for the rest of your natural life."

"I'm sorry. My behavior was ill-advised. I apologize. It won't happen again."

"I hope not because I meant what I said about the cops. Oh, and one other thing, tell your little colleen that I'd appreciate a bonus when she collects that $175,000 from her mother's estate. It needn't be much. Twenty-five thousand sounds like a nice neat figure."

"Ridiculous. First you accuse me or murder, then you want me to strong arm my fiancé. I really can't do that," Pfieffer says. "It's her money, not mine."

"But, Dylan, you are so persuasive and really it's cheap at the price since she won't have to think about those ghastly visiting hours at Quentin every Sunday."

I smile and get up, tossing a twenty on the table.

"I've lost my appetite as I'm sure you have as well," I say. "I'm going to make a short pit stop at the loo, walk a half-block to my car parked up the street and then head home to my loving wife. Let's stay in touch."

I turn and head toward the rest rooms, leaving Pfieffer behind. I am counting on the fact that he will leave the restaurant before I do.

Several minutes later I step out into the cool night air. Pfieffer was no longer on the premises. I look around. No sign of him. My gaze moves up the street to my Bentley which I have parked directly below a street lamp. Pfieffer knows the car and a blind man couldn't miss it in its pool of light. I walk toward it. I'm about to slip my key into the lock when I hear his voice behind me. He's been lurking in the shadows.

"Climb in, get behind the wheel and place your hands in your lap. Don't do anything stupid or I will be forced to shoot you here and now."

"As opposed to what, ten minutes from now?" I ask.

"In the car, Mr. Bernardi. Nobody likes a wise guy."

"My wife doesn't seem to mind," I reply.

He jabs the barrel of his gun into the small of my back. As Yogi Berra once famously said, it's deja vu all over again. I get into the car, settle behind the steering wheel, hands in my lap. I hear the rear door open and Pfieffer get in.

"What now?" I ask.

"Drive," he says.

"I don't think so," I say. "We've done this routine once before. It's not a lot of fun."

"Neither is a bullet in the back of your head."

"Are you threatening to kill me?"

"Isn't that fairly obvious, Mr. Bernardi?"

"Yes, but I just wanted to get it on the record."

"Record? What record? What are you talking about?"

And at that moment I lean on my horn and it blares loudly in every direction.

"What the hell are you doing? Are you crazy? Stop!"

And I do stop just as soon as Cosmo pulls up alongside my car, boxing me in. He and two of his men, one of them being Gunnar Larsen, clamber out of his car, guns drawn and all pointed at Dylan Pfieffer. I check him out in my rear view mirror. His eyes are wide and unfocused, a deer caught in the headlights.

A length of duct tape is used to cuff Pfieffer's hands behind his back and then he is dumped into the back of Cosmo's car. Gunnar slides in next to him for company on the ride across the hill to the Van Nuys police station. I follow in the Bentley.

Pete Rodriguez is not there. He is home for the evening but he returns when he learns that we have brought him a murderer. Whether this is out of curiosity or he is intent on chewing me out for continuing to involve myself in the Cummings murder, I do not know. I do know that he is exceedingly irritable because his evening at home has been disrupted and most of his anger is directed at me and not Cosmo who is sitting beside me.

Over Pfieffer's lawyerly objections, Pete listens to the voice activated tape I have made with my Phillips compact cassette recorder, secreted in my jacket pocket. Despite my best efforts I did not succeed in actually eliciting a confession at the Derby, a flaw which Pete is quick to point out. However there is no doubt that I was threatened with death while being held at gunpoint in my car and Pete is quick to charge him with several sections of California's penal statutes involving threats and endangerment. There is a slight problem of jurisdiction but Pete chooses to ignore it.

And that's when the phone rings. Pete picks up.

"Rodriguez." Listening. "Who?" More. "Yes, Superintendent, how can I help you?" More. "Mr. Stryker? Yes, he's here. I'll put him on." He hands the phone to Cosmo. "Damned Irish. Can't understand a thing they say," Pete mutters.

Cosmo takes the phone and immediately gets involved in a long-winded conversation which is mostly cryptic but obviously involves some sort of crime in Belfast. Finally he signs off and returns the phone to Pete. Throughout I have been carefully watching Dylan Pfieffer.

"That was Chief Superintendent Seamus Ryan with the Police Service of Northern Ireland." Cosmo says. "He's flying in tomorrow before noon with extradition papers involving Mr. Pfieffer."

"Me? What for?" Pfieffer says in a panic.

"Good question, Cosmo," Pete says,"what's the charge?"

"It has to do with an old lady who died in a nursing home. The mother of Mr. Pfieffer's fiancé. I didn't get all of it but there was an exhumation and a belated autopsy and also an eyewitness. I'm sure the Super will fill us in as soon as he arrives."

"Bollocks!" Pfieffer sputters. "I'm not involved in any murder, here, there or anywhere!"

"Maybe not," Cosmo shrugs. "But it seems they're coming to get you."

"Well, he'll be here," Pete says. "I can hold him without bail for seventy-two hours before arraignment on the endangerment charges."

He punches the intercom button and summons an officer to take Pfieffer to a holding cell. After Pfeiffer's been led out, Cosmo says to Pete, "I don't mean to step on your toes, Pete. I was acting on behalf of Robert Wagner and, well, we'd talked about the low profile thing."

"No problem, Cosmo," Pete says. "When Ryan arrives, let's see what he's got." Then he turns to me.

"Just this once, Joe, I'm not going to tell Bunny what you've been up to but I'm warning you as an officer of the law and begging you as a friend, stay out of police affairs. If I get popped I get a stately funeral complete with an honor guard and an American flag. You get a granite headstone and a few dozen people who'll weep over your grave for a few minutes and then get on with their lives. Yvette and Bunny deserve more."

I nod and tell him I agree and except for a couple of loose ends that still have to be tied off, I am going to cooperate.

Cosmo and I walk out into the crisp night air. It's just past ten o'clock. Time I got home to see my wife. I smile at Cosmo and he smiles back.

"One of us needs to fill in Ray Giordano," I say.

"He's on board," Cosmo says. "One of his paralegals is handling the paperwork."

"See you here tomorrow?" I ask him.

"I wouldn't miss this for the world," he replies, two men sharing a secret, and then we part and go to our cars and head for home.

A short time later I pull into the driveway and cut the engine. As soon as I walk in the kitchen door, my daughter comes flying at me from nowhere and I scoop her up in my arms. Easy enough when she was four. At twelve she's a load.

"Daddy!" she shrieks gleefully.

"Whoa!" I laugh. "What are you doing up at this hour of the night, princess?"

"My idea," Bunny says appearing in the doorway. "She hasn't seen you in two days and was starting to forget what you looked like."

I nod and then wink at Yvette.

"So how do I look?" I ask.

"Like a stud!" she giggles.

"And who taught you that word?" I ask.

"Cindy Kane. Why? Is it a dirty word?"

"Absolutely not. I'm very flattered. Not too many of us forty-six year old studs around these days." I ease her to the ground before my back gives out. "So what do you say, how about an ice cream party and you can tell me what's been going on in your life."

She beams and the three of us raid the refrigerator in search of rocky road, chocolate swirl and cherry vanilla. Yvette has been elected one of the sixth grade hall monitors. She got a B+ on a math test and a boy named Jacob Stern has asked her to go roller skating on Saturday with him and some of his friends.

"And what did you tell him?" I ask.

"I said I had to ask my Daddy."

"Do you want to go?"

"Sure. But he's Jewish."

"So what?" I tell her. "So are you. Half-Jewish anyway."

She nods.

"Some of the kids at school say things, about the Jewish kids."

"Bad things?"

"Not nice."

"And what do you say?"

"Nothing."

"Are you afraid?"

"Not really. I don't want to stir up trouble."

"If trouble broke out, it wouldn't be you that caused it, Yvette."

"I guess not."

"Do they know that you are Jewish?"

"I don't think so."

"But maybe if they found out, they might not like you as much as they used to."

"Maybe not."

I nod thoughtfully.

"Look, Yvette, it would be easy enough for me to tell you what to think and how to behave but I'm not going to do that. Two things. If your so-called friends turned their backs on you because you were Jewish, they weren't really worth having them as friends to begin with. The other thing is, every time someone makes a snotty remark about Jews, go find one of the Jewish kids, boy or girl, and sit down and talk with them. Doesn't matter about what. Just make it a point to show that hate is not a part of who you are. And finally, by all means, go roller skating with Jacob and his friends this weekend. You'll probably have a wonderful time."

"Right!" she says spooning out a huge glob of rocky road.

A half hour later Bunny and I tuck her in bed and go out into the hallway, closing her door behind us. Bunny smiles and takes me in her arms.

"Nice going, Daddy," she says quietly.

"About time, don't you think?" I say and in that moment I really understand what Pete and Aaron and the others have been saying to me. I have been given two very special gifts. I have no right to jeopardize them. Time to reassess how I am spending my life.

CHAPTER SEVENTEEN

The first rays of sunlight are forcing their way into our bedroom through the venetian blinds. I don't need a clock to tell me it's not yet six o'clock as I slowly and noiselessly slip from beneath the covers and pad toward the bathroom.

"Where are you going?" Bunny asks, her head half covered by sheets.

"Bathroom."

"And?"

"I thought I'd put in a couple of hours at the typewriter before breakfast."

"I thought you were blocked."

"I was but Sam escaped the warehouse by leaping into the Seine, then climbing aboard a *bateaux mouches* dinner cruise and disguising himself as a busboy."

"Sounds exciting."

"It is."

"You made a good start last night, Joe. Keep it up. Breakfast with me and Yvette. Eight o'clock sharp."

"Set your watch by me," I grin as I duck into the bathroom for a cold wakeup shower. My head's been twisting and turning all night as the pages that follow Sam's escape from the hungry horde of rats jell vividly in my brain. I can't wait to get it down on paper and once in my office the words, the sentences and the paragraphs gush onto the blank white sheets. Suddenly remembering my promise I glance up at the wall. My Mickey Mouse clock reads three minutes to eight. Much as I need to continue, my word is my word and I throw the dust cover over my trusty Smith-Corona and head downstairs.

Yvette is digging into a bowl of Kix and Bunny is nibbling on dry toast and sipping black coffee. Bridget is so startled to see me that she starts to fix my favorite, french toast and sausage. Bunny is so astounded that I've kept my promise that she doesn't object to the sausage. Having opened the door on Jacob Stern the night before, Yvette now proceeds to tell me all about him. His father is a doctor, his mother is a college professor and Jacob is the smartest boy in his school. He is also on the school basketball team because at five ten, he is the tallest boy in the class. He is also very good looking and tells funny stories. She goes on like this for several minutes and I am beginning to wonder if there might be an engagement ring upstairs hidden in her sock drawer. Bunny keeps throwing me knowing glances. She is thoroughly enjoying this. Finally Yvette races out the door to catch the school bus and I can breathe again.

Bunny smiles.

"Twelve is just the beginning. Wait until she turns thirteen and starts growing boobs."

Somehow I manage to smile back.

A few minutes later Bunny heads upstairs to change for work. I am sopping up the last of the maple syrup when the phone rings. I pick up. Glenda Mae is on the line.

"There's a woman here wants to see you," she says.

"Name?"

"Marigold Something-or-other. She wants your home address."

"Did you give it to her?"

"Did I seem demented the last time I saw you?"

"Hang onto her. I'll be there in thirty minutes."

Actually I make it in twenty-seven.

"She's in the conference room," Glenda Mae tells me when I walk into her office. "I gave her a mug of coffee and today's Variety."

"Exciting."

"Need me?"

"Not yet,"

"I'm here."

"I'll let you know."

I find her sitting at the far end of the mahogany trestle table that dominates the conference room. Today's Variety sits unread in the middle of the table. Her coffee mug is still full and she is staring off into space. She turns in my direction as I approach and sit in a chair next to hers. Her eyes are red from crying, her complexion grey from fear.

"I remembered the name of your office from that card you tried to give me." I nod. "I'm sorry," she continues, "about what Dylan put you through. That's not him. Not him at all, Mr. Bernardi. Guns and stuff. What came over him? Tell me that."

"Fear," I say.

"Fear? Him afraid of you? What for? Makes no sense."

"Maybe you should ask him."

"Can't. They won't let me see him. It's true then? He put a gun to your head?"

"He did."

"Jesus, Mary and Joseph," she mutters quietly under her breath. "Not like him. Not like him at all. Why did he do it?"

"To keep me quiet, Marigold. I know things. I know things about him that can put him in deep trouble."

"I can't believe that."

"Well, it's true."

"Tell me."

"Better that he tells you. You won't believe me." I hesitate, looking over at this pathetic waif. "Tell me, Marigold, what do you know about Dylan? I mean, really know."

"I know he's the first man ever to treat me like a woman. I know I love him. We're going to be married. Or at least we were." She gazes at me for a few moments. "I have no pride, Mr. Bernardi. I've come here to beg. Please, drop the charges against him. I swear by all that is holy, such a thing will never happen again."

"I think it's out of my hands, Marigold. Even if I wanted to, I don't think I can."

"You could. I know you could." Her tone is desperate.

"Marigold, you're not my daughter but even so I'm going to give you some fatherly advice. No matter how much you may think you love this man, you really don't know enough about him to commit for the rest of your life. I suggest you back away and keep an open mind, listen to what is said, judge him not with your heart but with your head."

"The things you won't tell me," she says,

"That's right."

"They are bad."

"Very bad," I say.

"I know he loves me. I can forgive him just about anything."

"I doubt he loves you, Marigold. You are wasted on him. Please listen to me. Open your eyes, use your brain."

She gets up from the table.

"I'm sorry I wasted your time," she says, "but I won't abandon him. Thank you for seeing me."

"Where are you going?" I ask.

"Back to the hotel. I don't know how long I can stay there. Dylan's been handling everything but money's tight."

"I'll drive you. Save you the cab fare."

"You don't have to."

"I know that," I say as I take her by the arm.

It's not that long a drive and for several minutes we sit in silence as she stares out the window holding in the desperate thoughts that must be plaguing her.

"You say money's tight," I venture. "Did Dylan mention anything about inheriting from your Mom."

"Inheriting? Inheriting what? A straw hat and a chipped tea set?"

"There might be something," I say. "Insurance, maybe."

"There's nothing. Dylan made it clear enough. Back in Belfast he's got his practice. After we're married we'll make do."

I glance over at her, curled up by the window. A nice enough girl but one of life's losers, prey for jackals like Dylan Pfieffer. If all goes well today, he won't be a problem but others like him roam the earth. Marriage in Vegas and then what? Pfieffer wed to a woman that doesn't know she could be worth nearly $200,000. Maybe she'll never find out or at least not before a fatal auto accident or a stumble down a long flight of stairs, leaving behind a husband that will grieve just as long as it takes for him to inherit his wife's holdings and not a minute later. No, this afternoon will be a moment of truth not only for Dylan Pfieffer but for Marigold Toms as well.

I pull up to the front entrance to the Biltmore and wish her luck as she gets out. She smiles and thanks me. I watch as the doorman holds the door for her and then she disappears from view. With a bit of luck, she will wake up tomorrow morning with no idea how lucky she is but someday she will.

Two o'clock rolls around. By now Cosmo has appeared at Pete Rodriguez's office and introduced him to Chief Superintendent Seamus Ryan of the Police Service of Northern Ireland. I'd considered being there but finally reasoned I would just be in the way and moreover, it would not be a good time to aggravate Pete about my continued meddling in his case. Whatever needs handling, Cosmo can handle.

A good plan but like all plans, subject to going awry and I begin to fret that this may be one of those times. By three o'clock I can stand it no more and I drive to Van Nuys to the police station. I am walking in the main entrance when I see them coming from the other direction: Cosmo, Pete and Superintendent Ryan. All three are smiling and it's pretty obvious to me that things have worked out.

Cosmo winks as I reach them.

"The situation has been resolved," he says.

"Meaning?"

"Meaning that Mr. Pfieffer has confessed to the slaying of Horatio Cummings."

"Proof?" I ask knowing that words alone won't convict him if he has a change of heart.

"He told us where to find the murder weapon. In the closet in his hotel room. We obtained a search warrant. Two detectives are on their way as we speak."

The man known as Seamus Ryan steps toward me with a smile, hand extended.

"Seamus Ryan," he says as we shake.

"Joe Bernardi," I say. "Sorry you had to make that long trip here for nothing, Superintendent, but I guess possession is nine-tenths of the law. In any case the gentleman will be locked up for a long, long time and really, what difference where, eh?"

"Well said," he smiles. With difficulty I suppress an urge to laugh out loud.

"Cosmo!"

A familiar voice rings out as we turn to see Bob Wagner hurrying toward us, eyeballing Cosmo. Ray Giordano is at his side.

"Your office said you were working on something." Wagner says. "Ray and I came down to see."

Wagner smiles at me and then at Pete Rodriquez and then as he turns to Seamus Ryan, a strange look crosses his face. He is puzzled.

"Bartlett? What are you doing here?"

'Seamus Ryan' shuffles his feet and tugs at his collar uncomfortably.

"Seamus Ryan," he says unconvincingly, putting out his hand.

"Horse puckey. What are you doing here, Bartlett? What's going on?"

Pete looks at Cosmo, then at me, his expression reflecting deep and serious suspicion. He looks next at 'Seamus'.

"Yes, Bartlett, or whatever the hell your name is, what is going on? I can't wait to find out."

CHAPTER EIGHTEEN

First and Twenty is a sports bar located on Victory Boulevard a few blocks away from LAPD headquarters. The owner, a two season veteran of the Raiders, started it when he realized he was a better businessman than he was a deep safety. Wisely he deduced that his name would probably not encourage patronage so he avoided using it. Nonetheless he has proved to be a warm and engaging host and the site is thriving.

It's five past five, Happy Hour, and we are gathered around a circular table nervously chatting as our drinks are served by a buxom young thing in a skimpy black and silver outfit. The only one not enjoying himself is Pete Rodriguez who acts like a man whose pocket has just been picked. He's waiting for someone to tell him why. I decide to elect myself.

"Okay, Pete, I know you're pissed and I guess you have a right to be but we, all of us, were determined to get Bob and Marian off the hook and it was pretty clear that only drastic measures were going to succeed."

Pete glares at me.

"Meaning make a fool of the cop and for God's sake, don't bring him into your confidence."

"Come on, Pete. We couldn't do that and you know it," Ray says.

Pete shoots him a disbelieving look.

"We? We? You were in on this, Ray?"

"Who the hell do you think drew up those phony extradition papers?"

Pete looks at me, totally at sea.

"Am I on duty now?" he asks.

"I don't know," I respond. "Are you?"

"I'm not sure I care," he says, taking a healthy swallow of his beer. I raise my glass. "Cheers," I say and follow suit. 'Superintendent Ryan' joins in. "*Sláinte*," he says.

"Whatever the hell that means?" Pete grouses.

"It's an Irish toast, boyo," he says.

"You mean you really are Irish?" Pete asks.

"Born and bred in County Wexford." he says, "before I came to America to make pirate pictures with Mr. Flynn. That was some years ago." He puts out his hand. "Bartlett McShane, Sergeant. A pleasure knowing you."

They shake.

"Likewise," Pete says between gritted teeth.

"He plays a pretty good cop, too, Sergeant," Wagner says.

"Or a magistrate or a doctor or a lawyer. I am a man of varied talents, sir," Bartlett says. "Me and Pat O'Brien."

Ray raps on the table for quiet.

"Gentlemen, we are gathered here to provide an explanation to our good friend, Sergeant Rodriguez, and Joe, since this dim-witted idea sprang full blown from your fevered brain why don't you do the honors?"

"I will, Ray, as long as we all understand that I never would have embarked on such a plan were I not sure I could find an equally dimwitted lawyer to go along with it."

A half-hearted dirty look from Ray, laughter from the others.

"Okay. So from the beginning this case is a mess. It's supposed to look like a killing in the commission of a robbery but it was so ineptly staged that such a possibility was never considered. Even Pete Rodriguez couldn't be so easily fooled."

Pete presents his middle finger for inspection.

"That means there is a motive in play and there are several possibilities. The most obvious is Garrison King but he's got a pretty tight alibi. Then there's Tony Trippi, the loan shark, but his business ethics dictate that he go after King, not Cummings, and beyond that, murder is not really an option, not if you want to get your money back. Marigold certainly had motive enough considering how badly Cummings had treated her mother and where there's Marigold, there is Dylan Pfieffer. They both had crappy alibis. She had gone to bed early in the hotel room. He claimed he'd had a few drinks in the bar and then went for a midnight walk. Forensic evidence? None except for two .45 slugs for which there was no corresponding gun. Fingerprints, none. Fiber evidence, none. Witnesses, none. Stymied. But because this case needed solving immediately to protect the Wagners, there was no time to wait for a lucky break to fall into our laps. So another approach was needed and I began to look at Old Faithful. Follow the money. This took on special relevance when I realized that the victim had just come into $200,000. After that it was paint by the numbers. Cummings dies and because they had drawn up mutual wills years earlier, Prunella gets the money. Prunella dies and Marigold gets the money. Pfieffer gets Marigold to say 'I do' in a chapel in Vegas and from that moment on, her days are numbered."

"And the fact that Pfieffer twice tried to muscle you sealed the deal, right, Joe?" Cosmo says.

"Just about, Cosmo. Also Pfieffer's little jaunt back to Belfast where he spent no more than two days, visiting Prunella although lying about it, and her dying a short time after he left the hospice, all very damning."

"Very damning indeed," Bartlett says, "which is why Mr. Bernardi contacted me to play a small part in his charade. I was only too happy to help for Mr. Wagner's sake. He has always treated me with great dignity."

"And much deserved, Bartlett," Bob says. "Few people treated this kid actor with as much friendship as you did."

"Cosmo, you were in the meeting. Take it from there."

"Well, Mr. McShane—Bartlett—played his part to a tee, alluding to fingerprints and witnesses and such and producing the extradition papers with such flair and certitude that Pfieffer must have felt the noose tightening around his neck. Remember that Pfieffer is a man of great ego and arrogance but at heart, not very bright. His failing legal practice attests to that.

"Anyway he starts babbling about getting a lawyer and fighting extradition and I tell him that he would be wasting his money and whatever funds he could get his hands on would be better spent defending himself on the charge of murder against Horatio Cummings. Even if he were to lose, here in California he might not face more than 20 to Life and parole was a possibility after about 13 years, maybe even sooner. California is like that. But if he lost in Belfast it would be the gallows within a week. Pfieffer profusely denied he was guilty of murder, here or there, and demanded to be released.

"As planned," Bartlett interjects, "I went into an indignant tirade demanding that Mr. Pfieffer be turned over to me so that Northern Island could mete out the most appropriate punishment for the callous murder of an enfeebled defenseless old woman. I was not about to leave his fate up to a jury of bleeding hearts more concerned with excusing his behavior than gaining justice for his victim. No, I made it clear that the Crown would not settle for half measures even if international relations had to be put at risk. It was at this point that a sly smile crossed Mr. Pfieffer's features as he reminded us all that just a month or two ago Great Britain had abolished the death penalty for all crimes, including first degree murder."

Ray chimes in. "I suggested to the gentleman that next time he is looking for information about the Crown's legal system that he read beyond the headline. Great Britain had indeed abolished capital punishment but Northern Ireland has not signed on and it is doubtful they ever will. It was at this point that Mr. Pfeiffer soiled his underwear and loudly proclaimed his guilt in the murder of Horatio Cummings. To his credit, Sergeant Rodriguez immediately informed him that a verbal confession alone would not be sufficient grounds to deny the extradition which is when Pfieffer acknowledged the existence of the murder weapon and where it could be found."

He turns to Pete with a smile. "Any questions, Sergeant? Anything else you need to know?"

"I guess not," Pete says. "We have his handwritten confession and the murder weapon. What else could I possibly need? It will. however, be some time before I can trust my good friend Joe Bernardi to level with me about such a trivial thing as a murder investigation."

"Actually, Pete," I say. "You could start tomorrow morning. I've given this scoop to Lou Cioffi and it's going to be first page Metro and all the credit for solving this bizarre killing has been given to Detective Sergeant Pedro Rodriguez of the Valley Homicide Division."

Pete perks up.

"Oh? Really?"

"Really."

"Well, in that case," he says raising his glass with a smile, "*Sláinte!*"

And Lou Cioffi does indeed have the story, or at least a version of it. I have given him everything and in return, he has agreed with me that it reads just as well without any specific mention of Bob or Marian Wagner. That's why I admire him as much as I do. He is a tenacious bulldog of a reporter but he also has good sense and a heart. This sets him worlds apart from many of his contemporaries who slant their material to mesh with their own world views instead of letting the facts speak for themselves. Maybe it's because he has so much in common with Tough Tony Trippi. They both splashed onto Omaha Beach to defend the American way of life including, in Lou's case, the sacred first amendment guaranteeing freedom of the press. Amazing these days how so many so-called journalists ignore it as if it were part and parcel of last night's garbage.

I get home just in time for supper with Bunny and Yvette. For the first time in many days I am relaxed and very much my old self. Bunny is quick to notice and I tell her that my fertile mind has saved Sam August from a fate worse than death. She seems to buy it and I am pretty sure none of my dear friends has let her know how I spent my afternoon.

I now have two loose ends to tie up, Bob Wagner as Sam August, and a pathetic Cockney waif named Marigold Toms who has been set adrift alone in the cruel and roiling sea called life. (Melville couldn't have described it better.) After dinner I call the Biltmore to find that she has checked out. On a hunch I ask for my faith-ful admirer, the desk clerk Lance, and discover that the hotel limo drove her to the airport for a red-eye flight to Belfast. I tell Bunny I have an errand to run that has nothing to do with mayhem, mys-tery or murder. I promise to be home by nine at the latest. She lets me go without a query.

I find Marigold huddled on a hard wooden bench near the gate for the midnight flight to Belfast. Her face is wan and she is staring off into space, as bewildered as she has ever been by the events that have turned her life inside out. As I sit down next to her, she turns to me and a faint smile crosses her lips.

"You were right, Mr. Bernardi. About Dylan, I mean," she says.

"I take no joy in it, Marigold."

"I think I must be very, very stupid."

"No, Dylan was very, very smart and you are not a worldly young lady. Take that as a compliment. That's how I mean it." She nods. "So, what are your plans?" I ask.

"Get a job, get on with my life. I have a cousin who will put me up for a while until I'm settled."

"You do know that you may have a lot of money coming some day."

"You mean the book thing."

"Yes. I know the producer. There is a good chance the film will never get made but this is Hollywood, a world where impossibilities often triumph over sanity and I may be dead wrong. I hope I am. $175,000 is a lot of money. In the meantime —" I reach into my jacket pocket and take out a check which I hand her. "I want you to take this to help get you through the first few weeks. Call it a loan. If the film comes through, pay me back. If not, I'll take a write-off."

She looks at the check.

"Two thousand dollars." She shakes her head. "I can't take this."

"Of course you can. Didn't I just say it was a loan?" I get to my feet. "I have to run. My little girl's at home waiting for me to tuck her in. Safe flight, Marigold. I'll be rooting for you."

I lean over and give her a peck on her cheek. She reaches up and puts her arms around my neck for the briefest of moments and then lets go. She has tears dribbling slowly down her cheeks. I wipe them away and then turn and leave. I doubt it will ever come to pass but I hope that in the future, if misfortune should befall Yvette and I were not around to rectify it, that some stranger would show her the same compassion that I have just shown Marigold Toms.

CHAPTER NINETEEN

Tonight we party.

It has been fourteen days since we unmasked the guilt of Dylan Pfieffer who now resides in the L.A. County jail awaiting his trial which won't actually be a trial but an allocution by him as to the circumstances of Horatio Cummings' murder. From there he will be taken to a California penal institution (I've been told Chino) where he will spend the next dozen years of his worthless life. This is provided he behaves himself. I'm hoping he doesn't. I'm hoping he smart mouths his way to at least 40 years and a boyfriend named Bruno.

But as I say, all of this is behind us and tonight we celebrate. Bunny, Yvette and I have accepted a very special invitation to attend the wrap party for 'Harper' which will be held on Stage 12 at the Warners studios. A wrap party is a gala held for the cast and crew of a motion picture immediately following the final day of shooting. Food is in abundance and wine and tears flow like Niagara. Co-workers pledge undying friendship and bemoan the loss of the camaraderie of the past several weeks. The truth is, tomorrow is another day, everyone heads off to a new job on a new film or goes home to wait for the phone to ring and torrid love affairs flame out like candles in a windstorm. Hollywood is more a land of transitory relationships than friendships, though the latter do exist, but they

collared shirt, Yvette in a skirt and cashmere sweater and pearl neck-
lace and Bunny looking almost, but not quite, like Rita Hayworth
in 'Gilda'. The gate guard directs us to a parking area near Stage 12
where a valet takes charge of the Bentley. The delivery doors have
been thrown wide open and as we approach I can hear the sounds of
laughter and a four or five piece combo playing 'Canadian Capers'.

As we start in I am aware that my daughter has stopped dead
in her tracks and is staring straight ahead, eyes wide and mouth
half open. I look and there is Edd Byrnes deep in conversation
with Shelley Winters. I suspect it's not Shelley that Yvette is staring at. I tug at Bunny's elbow and head nod toward Yvette. Bunny
catches on and raises her eyes to heaven. Edd Byrnes,'Kookie' on
the Warners television show '77 Sunset Strip', is apparently catnip to
the country's female teen population and Yvette is no exception. It's
going to be a long night, I tell Bunny under my breath. She concurs.

I make a beeline for one of the four bars and order a Perrier for
Bunny, a cherry coke for Yvette and an orange Nehi for me. Out
of the corner of my eye I catch Arthur Hill hurrying toward us and
before I can intercede he has my wife in an affectionate clinch. This
goes back almost fourteen years to a time when Bunny was in New
York, working as a junior editor for *Colliers* magazine and Arthur
was a struggling young actor, several years before his triumphant
Tony win in 'Who's Afraid of Virginia Woolf'. Arthur's wife Peggy
slides in next to me and tosses a gentle elbow into my ribs. I smile
at her. She smiles back. Graciously we tolerate this display of auld
lang syne between our spouses who eventually come up for air. We
chat for a few minutes, always fun with Arthur who is a soft spoken
highly erudite man. We break up when Arthur spots Jack Warner
coming in and excusing himself, hustles off to pay his respects and
perhaps wangle further employment. The life of a Hollywood actor,
even a successful one, is often a precarious one.

Bunny and I drift toward the huge banquet table in the center of the room. Dishes and platters are piled high with shrimp, crab legs, lobster tails, canapés, salads, roast beef, turkey and a half dozen varieties of pasta. Edd Byrnes is now chatting with Tony Curtis and Janet Leigh. Directly behind Byrnes is my daughter who is still staring up at him with cow-like adoring eyes. Tomorrow at school, Yvette will have plenty to talk about with the other girls in her class.

From the moment we walked onto the soundstage I have been scanning the premises for Bob Wagner and now I spot him, just arriving, with Marian and the two boys in tow. At that moment he also spies me and waves, I wave back and watch as he gives his wife a quick kiss on the cheek and then hurries in my direction.

Wagner's face is haggard as he reaches me.

"Joe, I am so sorry. I don't know what to say."

"Say? Say what?"

"Haven't you talked to Walter?" he asks with a frown.

"He put a call into me but we haven't connected," I say.

"Damn!" he mutters under his breath.

"What is it, Bob? What's going on?"

He grabs me by the elbow and starts to steer me to one of the huge open delivery doors.

"Let's take a walk where it's not so crowded."

A few moments later we're outside. The sun is still up and the air is still warm as he pulls me across the alley to the entrance to Stage 13. The sounds of merriment are dimly in the distance.

"First of all, Joe, I had no idea. No, that's not right but I swear I had forgotten all about it."

"Forgotten all about what? Bob, you're not making any sense."

"The commitment. The television pilot."

Now it's my turn to frown. I definitely do not like the sound of this.

"Years ago I wanted a part in a McQueen movie called 'The War Lover'."

"I remember it," I say.

"I thought it was going to be a significant film. A career maker. A stepping stone to the kind of parts that were going to Newman and Brando and Monty Clift. Just once it would have been nice to turn on the television in January and find out I'd been nominated. Maybe a supporting Oscar. Anything that had the aura of prestige about it. I don't remember the details but someone with muscle got me the number two part to McQueen and in return I signed an option for a television series to be exercised at some time in the future.

"And?"

"It's been exercised. The guy, and I honestly do not remember his name, developed a script with a top television writer, Roland Kibbee, and took it to Universal. Universal took it to ABC and they jumped at it, especially with me attached, don't ask me why."

"Crap," I say quietly.

"I know, I know," Bob says, "I begged my manager to get me out of it, he says no can do. Look, Joe, this pilot, it's nothing special. Another typical network pilot with a gimmick and not much else. I play a jewel thief that goes to work for the cops so I won't have to go to jail. Clever, huh? It's called 'It Takes a Thief', probably because Cary Grant and Grace Kelly already used 'To Catch a Thief'. You know what I think, Joe?"

"No, what do you think, Bob?" I ask, unable to keep my annoyance from seeping through.

"I think this pilot doesn't have a prayer in hell of going to series. I think I am going to pick up a nice piece off change for 20 days work and when the network schedules are announced a few weeks from now, this thief thing will be gathering dust on a shelf in some editing room and you and I can start bringing Sam August to life. Can you hold off for a few weeks, Joe? Can you give me that much?"

He looks so stricken I feel sorry for him. It's no act. Bob Wagner sees himself as a movie idol, not some nice-try near-miss pretty boy that Hollywood has passed over.

"I can wait, Bob," I say. "So can Walter, I think we'll be drama-tizing the adventures of Sam August for many years to come. As Bogey said to Claude Rains in the final scene of 'Casablanca', 'Louie, I think this is the beginning of a beautiful friendship.'"

A look of relief passes across his face and he reaches out and embraces me with a slap on the back.

"I won't let you down, Joe. Promise," he says."Come on, let's go find the ladies and party."

We head back, neither of us really happy. Despite my words to the contrary, I find myself on a teeter-totter trying to keep my balance. What had once been a sure thing is now nothing of the kind. With Sam it's always something getting in the way. Maybe I'm overreacting but I don't think so. As for Bob I know damned well he has no great desire to become a television star. Yes, a hit show can make him a millionaire overnight but he has his sights set higher than that.

How will this all play out? I have absolutely no idea.

Lost in my thoughts I walk back onto the soundstage only to be confronted by my daughter who is doing the Twist with Edd Byrnes. At least I think it's the Twist. It could be the Watusi or the Crushed Pineapple or whatever. All these dances, I can't keep them straight and a bothersome sacroiliac hinders me from exploring them. No matter. The sparkle in Yvette's eyes and the grin on her face have made this evening all worthwhile.

The music suddenly segues into a two-four version of 'Stardust' and Bunny is a few feet away chatting with Marian. I grab her by the elbow, spin her around and take her in my arms. Now the sparkle is in my eyes and the grin on my face and I am reminded of Scarlett O'Hara's famous line at the end of 'Gone With The Wind'. Tomorrow is another day.

THE END

AUTHOR'S NOTE

Like its predecessors, this installment of The Hollywood Murder Mysteries is pure fiction and other than the fact that Robert Wagner did co-star with Paul Newman and others in "Harper" none of the events, save one, involving Wagner and/or his wife Marian have a scintilla of truth. There was no Horatio Cummings, no Regal King Productions, no Garrison King and to the best of my knowledge Marian Wagner never had to endure the harassment of a stalker. Having segued Joe Bernardi into a new career as a novelist, the author found himself faced with a lot of 'what if's?', one of which was who would be ideal to portray his stalwart hero, Sam August, in a feature film. Bob Wagner became the perfect choice but involving Mr. Wagner in the filming of the picture without also involving him in murder, suspense and intrigue violates everything this series of novels is about. Hence, a very, very fictional storyline. In 1967 Wagner shot the pilot for "It Takes a Thief" and it was immediately picked up for series by ABC. A certifiable hit, it lasted for three seasons. It was followed soon after by a three year run of "Switch" and eventually a five year run on 'Hart to Hart" co-starring Stephanie Powers. As his highly popular television career thrived and his bank account ballooned, Wagner's movie career waned and he was no longer considered for major parts in top line motion pictures. His marriage to Marian ended in 1971 and the following year he re-married his first wife, actress Natalie Wood. She drowned in a boating accident under mysterious circumstances in 1981 and Wagner remained unmarried until 1990 when he wed, and is still married to, Jill St. John. Today, he continues to work, mainly in television, and his fans are legion.

ABOUT THE AUTHOR

Peter S. Fischer is a former
television writer-producer
who currently lives in the
Monterey Bay area of Central
California. He is a co-creator
of "Murder, She Wrote" for
which he wrote over 40 scripts.
Among his other credits are
a dozen "Columbo" episodes
and a season helming "Ellery
Queen." He has also written and produced several TV mini-series
and Movies of the Week. In 1985 he was awarded an Edgar by the
Mystery Writers of America. In addition to four EMMY nomi-
nations, two Golden Globe Awards for Best TV series, and an
Anthony Award from the Boucheron, he has received the IBPA
award for the Best Mystery Novel of the Year, a Bronze Medal
from the Independent Publishers Association and an Honorable
Mention from the San Francisco Festival for his first novel.

Available at Amazon.com

www.petersfischer.com

PRAISE FOR THE HOLLYWOOD MURDER MYSTERIES

Jezebel in Blue Satin

In this stylish homage to the detective novels of Hollywood's Golden Age, a press agent stumbles across a starlet's dead body and into the seamy world of scheming players and morally bankrupt movie moguls.....An enjoyable fast-paced whodunit from opening act to final curtain.
—Kirkus Reviews

Fans of golden era Hollywood, snappy patter and Raymond Chandler will find much to like in Peter Fischer's murder mystery series, all centered on old school studio flak, Joe Bernardi, a happy-go-lucky war veteran who finds himself immersed in tough situations.....The series fills a niche that's been superseded by explosions and violence in too much of popular culture and even though jt's a world where men are men and women are dames, its glimpses at an era where the facade of glamour and sophistication hid an uglier truth are still fun to revisit.
—2012 San Francisco Book Festival, Honorable Mention

Jezebel in Blue Satin, set in 1947, finds movie studio publicist Joe Bernardi slumming it at a third rate motion picture house running on large egos and little talent. When the ingenue from the film referenced in the title winds up dead, can Joe uncover the killer before he loses his own life? Fischer makes an effortless transition from TV mystery to page turner, breathing new life into the film noir hard boiled detective tropes. Although not a professional sleuth, Joe's evolution from everyman into amateur private eye makes sense; any bad publicity can cost him his job so he has to get to the bottom of things.
—ForeWord Review

exist despite the filmmaking process and not because of it.

Overwhelmed by the prospect of actually meeting Paul Newman, Bunny had insisted she buy a new gown for the occasion. I suggested this was not necessary, that wrap parties were pretty casual but if it would make her happy, go ahead just as long as she realized that she would be the only woman there in a gown. Upon reflection she settled for a very sexy red silk sheath. I neglected to tell her that she would also have the pleasure of meeting Paul's wife, Joanne Woodward.

The last two days have been more than interesting. On Tuesday I received a letter from Marigold telling me that she had found a wonderful job as a receptionist at a real estate office and two of the salesmen were good looking and single and both had asked her out to dinner and the cinema. Separately, of course. She had enclosed my two thousand dollar check, uncashed. The cousin had taken her in and refused to take any money until she was on her feet. I have good feelings about Marigold's future even though she is not going to see any part of that $175,000 option money from Garrison King. I'll tell you how I know.

It was a very tiny item buried on page 11 of today's Hollywood Reporter. Garrison's ace-in-the-hole, that nubile young actress with the impeccable filmdom pedigree, has suddenly opted for romance over 'The Enchanted Palazzo", married a talented French filmmaker and fled the States for Paris where she will star for him in a movie based on a long forgotten musty old French novel. Looks like 'Revenge of the Gila Monster' is going to be Garrison King's sole entry in next year's Oscar competition.

I also get a call from Walter Mirisch on my answering machine but when I try to get back to him, I was told by his secretary that he left for his getaway home in Montecito and he'll call me first thing in the morning.

We leave for the studio at six, me in a sports jacket and an open

We Don't Need No Stinking Badges

A *thrilling mystery packed with Hollywood glamour, intrigue and murder, set in 1948 Mexico.....Although the story features many famous faces (Humphrey Bogart, director John Huston, actor Walter Huston and novelist B. Traven, to name a few), the plot smartly focuses on those behind the scenes. The big names aren't used as gimmicks—they're merely planets for the story to rotate around. Joe Bernardi is the star of the show and this fictional tale in a real life setting (the actual set of 'Treasure of the Sierra Madre' was also fraught with problems) works well in Fischer's sure hands....A smart clever Mexican mystery.*

—Kirkus Reviews

A former TV writer continues his old-time Hollywood mystery series, seamlessly interweaving fact and fiction in this drama that goes beyond the genre's cliches. "We Don't Need No Stinking Badges" again transports readers to post WWII Tinseltown inhabited by cinema publicist Joe Bernardi... Strong characterization propels this book. Toward the end the crosses and double-crosses become confusing, as seemingly inconsequential things such as a dead woman who was only mentioned in passing in the beginning now become matters on which the whole plot turns (but) such minor hiccups should not deter mystery lovers, Hollywood buffs or anyone who adores a good yarn.

—ForeWord Review

Peter S. Fischer has done it again—he has put me in a time machine and landed me in 1948. He has written a fast paced murder mystery that will have you up into the wee hours reading. If you love old movies, then this is the book for you.

—My Shelf. Com

This is a complex, well-crafted whodunit all on its own. There's plenty of action and adventure woven around the mystery and the characters are fully fashioned. The addition of the period piece of the 1940's filmmaking and the inclusion of big name stars as supporting characters is the whipped cream and cherry on top. It all comes together to make an engaging and fun read.

—Nyssa, Amazon Customer Review

Love Has Nothing to Do With It

Fischer's experience shows in 'Love Has Nothing To Do With It', an homage to film noir and the hard-boiled detective novel. The story is complicated... but Fischer never loses the thread. The story is intricate enough to be intriguing but not baffling....Joe Bernardi's swagger is authentic and entertaining. Overall he is a likable sleuth with the dogged determination to uncover the truth.... While the outcome of the murder is an unknown until the final pages of the current title, we do know that Joe Bernardi will survive at least until 1950, when further adventures await him in the forthcoming 'Everybody Wants an Oscar'.

—Clarion Review

A stylized, suspenseful Hollywood whodunit set in 1949....Goes down smooth for murder-mystery fans and Old Hollywood junkies.

—Kirkus Review

The Hollywood Murder Mysteries just might make a great Hallmark series. Let's give this book: The envelope please: FIVE GOLDEN OSCARS.

—Samfreene, Amazon Customer Review

The writing is fantastic and, for me, the topic was a true escape into our past entertainment world. Expect it to be quite different from today's! But that's why readers will enjoy visiting Hollywood as it was in the past. A marvelous concept that hopefully will continue up into the 60s and beyond. Loved it!

—GABixlerReviews

The Unkindness of Strangers

Winner of the Benjamin Franklin Award
for Best Mystery Book of 2012
by the Independent Book Publisher's Association.

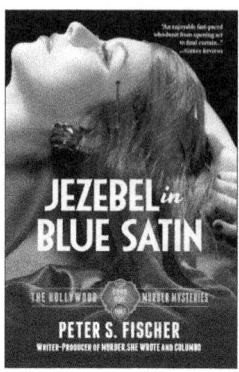

Book One—1947
JEZEBEL IN BLUE SATIN

WWII is over and Joe Bernardi has just returned home after three years as a war correspondent in Europe. Married in the heat of passion three weeks before he shipped out, he has come home to find his wife Lydia a complete stranger. It's not long before Lydia is off to Reno for a quickie divorce which Joe won't accept. Meanwhile he's been hired as a publicist by third rate movie studio, Continental Pictures. One night he enters a darkened sound stage only to discover the dead body of ambitious, would-be actress Maggie Baumann. When the police investigate, they immediately zero in on Joe as the perp. Short on evidence they attempt to frame him and almost succeed. Who really killed Maggie? Was it the over-the-hill actress trying for a comeback? Or the talentless director with delusions of grandeur? Or maybe it was the hapless leading man whose career is headed nowhere now that the "real stars" are coming back from the war. There is no shortage of suspects as the story speeds along to its exciting and unexpected conclusion.

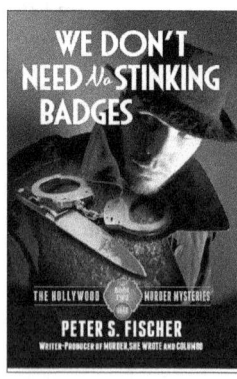

Book Two—1948
WE DON'T NEED NO STINKING BADGES

Joe Bernardi is the new guy in Warner Brothers' Press Department so it's no surprise when Joe is given the unenviable task of flying to Tampico, Mexico, to bail Humphrey Bogart out of jail without the world learning about it. When he arrives he discovers that Bogie isn't the problem. So-called accidents are occurring daily on the set, slowing down the filming of "The Treasure of the Sierra Madre" and putting tempers on edge. Everyone knows who's behind the sabotage. It's the local Jefe who has a finger in every illegal pie. But suddenly the intrigue widens and the murder of one of the actors throws the company into turmoil. Day by day, Joe finds himself drawn into a dangerous web of deceit, dupliciity and blackmail that nearly costs him his life.

Book Three—1949
LOVE HAS NOTHING TO DO WITH IT

Joe Bernardi's ex-wife Lydia is in big, big trouble. On a Sunday evening around midnight she is seen running from the plush offices of her one- time lover, Tyler Banks. She disappears into the night leaving Banks behind, dead on the carpet with a bullet in his head. Convinced that she is innocent, Joe enlists the help of his pal, lawyer Ray Giordano, and bail bondsman Mick Clausen, to prove Lydia's innocence, even as his assignment to publicize Jimmy Cagney's comeback movie for Warner's threatens to take up all of his time. Who really pulled the trigger that night? Was it the millionaire whose influence reached into City Hall? Or the not so grieving widow finally freed from a loveless marriage. Maybe it was the partner who wanted the business all to himself as well as the new widow. And what about the mysterious envelope, the one that disappeared and everyone claims never existed? Is it the key to the killer's identity and what is the secret that has been kept hidden for the past forty years?

Book Four—1950
EVERYBODY WANTS AN OSCAR

After six long years Joe Bernardi's novel is at last finished and has been shipped to a publisher. But even as he awaits news, fingers crossed for luck, things are heating up at the studio. Soon production will begin on Tennessee Williams' "The Glass Menagerie" and Jane Wyman has her sights set on a second consecutive Academy Award. Jack Warner has just signed Gertrude Lawrence for the pivotal role of Amanda and is positive that the Oscar will go to Gertie. And meanwhile Eleanor Parker, who has gotten rave reviews for a prison picture called "Caged" is sure that 1950 is her year to take home the trophy. Faced with three very talented ladies all vying for his best efforts, Joe is resigned to performing a monumental juggling act. Thank God he has nothing else to worry about or at least that was the case until his agent informed him that a screenplay is floating around Hollywood that is a dead ringer for his newly completed novel. Will the ladies be forced to take a back seat as Joe goes after the thief that has stolen his work, his good name and six years of his life?

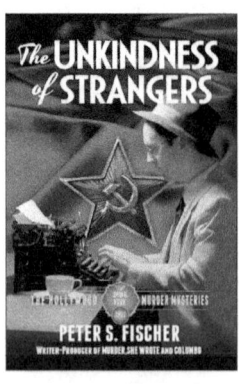

Book Five—1951
THE UNKINDNESS OF STRANGERS

Warner Brothers is getting it from all sides and Joe Bernardi seems to be everybody's favorite target. "A Streetcar Named Desire" is unproducible, they say. Too violent, too seedy, too sexy, too controversial and what's worse, it's being directed by that well-known pinko, Elia Kazan. To make matters worse, the country's number one hate monger, newspaper columnist Bryce Tremayne, is coming after Kazan with a vengeance and nothing Joe can do or say will stop him. A vicious expose column is set to run in every Hearst paper in the nation on the upcoming Sunday but a funny thing happens Friday night. Tremayne is found in a compromising condition behind the wheel of his car, a bullet hole between his eyes. Come Sunday and the scurrilous attack on Kazan does not appear. Rumors fly. Kazan is suspected but he's not the only one with a motive. Consider:

Elvira Tremayne, the unloved widow. Did Tremayne slug her one time too many?

Hubbell Cox, the flunky whose homosexuality made him a target of derision.

Willie Babbitt, the muscle. He does what he's told and what he's told to do is often unpleasant.

Jenny Coughlin, Tremayne's private secretary. But how private and what was her secret agenda?

Jed Tompkins, Elvira's father, a rich Texas cattle baron who had only contempt for his son-in-law.

Boyd Larabee, the bookkeeper, hired by Tompkins to win Cox's confidence and report back anything he's learned.

Annie Petrakis, studio makeup artist. Tremayne destroyed her lover. Has she returned the favor?

Book Six—1952
NICE GUYS FINISH DEAD

Ned Sharkey is a fugitive from mob revenge. For six years he's been successfully hiding out in the Los Angeles area while a $100, 000 contract for his demise hangs over his head. But when Warner Brothers begins filming "The Winning Team", the story of Grover Cleveland Alexander, Ned can't resist showing up at the ballpark to reunite with his old pals from the Chicago Cubs of the early 40's who have cameo roles in the film. Big mistake. When Joe Bernardi, Warner Brothers publicity guy, inadvertently sends a press release and a photo of Ned to the Chicago papers, mysterious people from the Windy City suddenly appear and a day later at break of dawn, Ned's body is found sprawled atop the pitcher's mound. It appears that someone is a hundred thousand dollars richer. Or maybe not. Who is the 22 year old kid posing as a 50 year old former hockey star? And what about Gordo Gagliano, a mountain of a man, who is out to find Ned no matter who he has to hurt to succeed? And why did baggy pants comic Fats McCoy jump Ned and try to kill him in the pool parlor? It sure wasn't about money. Joe , riddled with guilt because the photo he sent to the newspapers may have led to Ned's death, finds himself embroiled in a dangerous game of who-dun-it that leads from L. A. 's Wrigley Field to an upscale sports bar in Altadena to the posh mansions of Pasadena and finally to the swank clubhouse of Santa Anita racetrack.

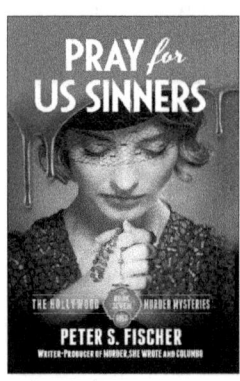

Book Seven–1953
PRAY FOR US SINNERS

Joe finds himself in Quebec but it's no vacation. Alfred Hitchcock is shooting a suspenseful thriller called "I Confess" and Montgomery Clift is playing a priest accused of murder. A marriage made in heaven? Hardly. They have been at loggerheads since Day One and to make matters worse their feud is spilling out into the newspapers. When vivacious Jeanne d'Arcy, the director of the Quebec Film Commisssion volunteers to help calm the troubled waters, Joe thinks his troubles are over but that was before Jeanne got into a violent spat with a former lover and suddenly found herself under arrest on a charge of first degree murder. Guilty or not guilty? Half the clues say she did it, the other half say she is being brilliantly framed. But by who? Fingers point to the crooked Gonsalvo brothers who have ties to the Buffalo mafia family and when Joe gets too close to the truth, someone tries to shut him up. . . permanently. With the Archbishop threatening to shut down the production in the wake of the scandal, Joe finds himself torn between two loyalties.

Book Eight–1954
HAS ANYBODY HERE SEEN WYCKHAM?

Everything was going smoothly on the set of "The High and the Mighty" until the cast and crew returned from lunch. With one exception. Wiley Wyckham, the bit player sitting in seat 24A on the airliner mockup, is among the missing, and without Wyckham sitting in place, director William Wellman cannot continue filming. A studio wide search is instituted. No Wyckham. A lookalike is hired that night, filming resumes the next day and still no Wyckham. Except that by this time, it's been discovered that Wyckham, a British actor, isn't really Wyckham at all but an imposter who may very well be an agent for the Russian government, The local police call in the FBI. The FBI calls in British counterintelligence. A manhunt for the missing actor ensues and Joe Bernardi, the picture's publicist, is right in the middle of the intrigue. Everyone's upset, especially John Wayne who is furious to learn that a possible Commie spy has been working in a picture he's producing and starring in. And then they find him . It's the dead of night on the Warner Brothers backlot and Wyckham is discovered hanging by his feet from a streetlamp, his body bloodied and tortured and very much dead. and pinned to his shirt is a piece of paper with the inscription "Sic Semper Proditor". (Thus to all traitors). Who was this man who had been posing as an obscure British actor? How did he smuggle

Book Seventeen—1963
CUE THE CROWS

How do you make a movie when the star of your dreams, eager to sign, is suddenly faced with a murder charge and could spend the rest of his life cooped up in San Quentin? Joe Bernardi, author, screenwriter and possibly a co-producer, has traveled north along the California coastline to Bodega Bay to hobnob with Rod Taylor who is filming Alfred Hitchcock's thriller, 'The Birds'. Rod is on the verge of signing the contract when a funny thing happens. The body of a young attractive redhead named Amanda Broome is found dead in the trunk of his Corvette. Taylor screams frame-up, even though Amanda has been stalking him for weeks and they had a violent and very public argument only hours before her body was discovered. Further filming of 'The Birds' is in jeopardy and so is the filming of Joe's movie based on his best-selling book. Looming large in the midst of this is Henrietta Boyle, a county attorney with gubernatorial ambitions and what better way to grease the path to the State House than to convict a famous movie star of homicide. But who else might have an interest in seeing Amanda dead? Perhaps her aunt, executrix of a trust fund which would have made Amanda a millionairess in a few short weeks. A definite possibility . Determined to prove Taylor innocent, Joe follows a trail that leads from a teen hangout in Palo Alto to the halls of academia to a posh country club where a triple A credit rating is the first requirement for membership. When a mysterious car tries to run Joe off the road into a deep and deadly crevasse in the hills above the Bay, he knows he's getting close to the truth but will the truth be revealed before Joe becomes buzzard bait?

himself into the country and what has he been up to? Has he been blackmailing an important higher-up in the film business and did the victim suddenly turn on him? Is the MI6 agent from London really who he says he is and what about the reporter from the London Daily Mail who seems to know all the right questions to ask as well all the right answers.

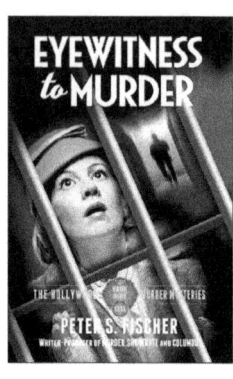

Book Nine—1955
EYEWITNESS TO MURDER

Go to New York? Not on your life. It's a lousy idea for a movie. A two year old black and white television drama? It hasn't got a prayer. This is the age of CinemaScope and VistaVision and stereophonic sound and yes, even 3-D. Burt Lancaster and Harold Hecht must be out of their minds to think they can make a hit movie out of "Marty". But then Joe Bernardi gets word that the love of his life, Bunny Lesher, is in New York and in trouble and so Joe changes his mind. He flies east to talk with the movie company and also to find Bunny and dig her out of whatever jam she's in. He finds that "Marty" is doing just fine but Bunny's jam is a lot bigger than he bargained for. She's being held by the police as an eyewitness to a brutal murder of a close friend in a lower Manhattan police station. Only a jammed pistol saved Bunny from being the killer's second victim and now she's in mortal danger because she knows what the man looks like and he's dead set on shutting her up. Permanently. Crooked lawyers, sleazy con artists and scheming businessmen cross Joe's path, determined to keep him from the truth and when the trail leads to the sports car racing circuit at Lime Rock in Connecticut, it's Joe who becomes the killer's prime target.

Book Ten—1956
A DEADLY SHOOT IN TEXAS

Joe Bernardi's in Marfa, Texas, and he's not happy. The tarantulas are big enough to carry off the cattle , the wind's strong enough to blow Marfa into New Mexico, and the temperature would make the Congo seem chilly. A few miles out of town Warner Brothers is shooting Edna Ferber's "Giant" with a cast that includes Rock Hudson, Elizabeth Taylor and James Dean and Jack Warner is paying through the nose for Joe's expertise as a publicist. After two days in Marfa Joe finds himself in a lonely cantina around midnight, tossing back a few cold ones, and being seduced by a gorgeous student young enough to be his daughter. The flirtation goes nowhere but the next morning little Miss Coed is found dead . And there's a problem. The coroner says she died between eight and nine o'clock. Not so fast, says Joe, who saw her alive as late as one a.m. When he points this out to the County Sheriff, all hell breaks loose and Joe becomes the target of some pretty ornery people. Like the Coroner and the Sheriff as well as the most powerful rancher in the county, his arrogant no-good son and his two flunkies, a crooked lawyer and a grieving father looking for justice or revenge, either one will do. Will Joe expose the murderer before the murderer turns Joe into Texas road kill? Tune in.

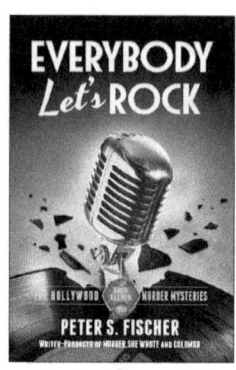

Book Eleven—1957
EVERYBODY LET'S ROCK

Big trouble is threatening the career of one of the country's hottest new teen idols and Joe Bernardi has been tapped to get to the bottom of it. Call it blackmail or call it extortion, a young woman claims that a nineteen year old Elvis Presley impregnated her and then helped arrange an abortion. There's a letter and a photo to back up her claim. Nonsense, says Colonel Tom Parker, Elvis's manager and mentor. It's a damned lie. Joe is not so sure but Parker is adamant. The accusation is a totally bogus and somebody's got to prove it. But no police can be involved and no lawyers. Just a whiff of scandal and the young man's future will be destroyed, even though he's in the midst of filming a movie that could turn him into a bona fide film star. Joe heads off to Memphis under the guise of promoting Elvis's new film and finds himself mired in a web of deceit and danger. Trusted by no one he searches in vain for the woman behind the letter, crossing paths with Sam Philips of Sun Records, a vindictive alcoholic newspaper reporter, a disgraced doctor with a seedy past, and a desperate con artist determined to keep Joe from learning the truth.

Book Twelve—1958
A TOUCH OF HOMICIDE

It takes a lot to impress Joe Bernardi. He likes his job and the people he deals with but nobody is really special. Nobody, that is, except for Orson Welles, and when Avery Sterling, a bottom feeding excuse for a producer, asks Joe's help in saving Welles from an industry-wide smear campaign, Joe jumps in, heedless that the pool he has just plunged into is as dry as a vermouthless martini. A couple of days later, Sterling is found dead in his office and the police immediately zero in on two suspects—Joe who has an alibi and Welles who does not. Not to worry, there are plenty of clues at the crime scene including a blood stained monogrammed handkerchief, a rejected screenplay, a pair of black-rimmed reading glasses, a distinctive gold earring and petals from a white carnation. What's more, no less than four people threatened to kill him in front of witnesses. A case so simple a two-year old could solve it but the cop on the case is a dimwit whose uncle is on the staff of the police commissioner. Will Joe and Orson solve the case before one of them gets arrested for murder? Will an out-of-town hitman kill one or both of them? Worst of all, will Orson leave town leaving Joe holding the proverbial bag?

Book Thirteen—1959
SOME LIKE 'EM DEAD

After thirteen years, the great chase is over and Joe Bernardi is marrying Bunny Lesher. After a brief weekend honeymoon, it'll be back to work for them both; Bunny at the Valley News where she has just been named Assistant Editor and Joe publicizing Billy Wilder's new movie, Some Like It Hot about two musicians hiding out from the mob in an all-girl band. It boasts a great script and a stellar cast that includes Tony Curtis, Jack Lemmon and Marilyn Monroe, so what could go wrong? Plenty and it starts with Shirley Davenport, Bunny's protege at the News, who has been assigned to the entertainment pages. To placate Bunny and against his better judgement Joe gives Shirley a press credential for the shoot and from the start, she is a destructive force, alienating cast and crew, including Billy Wilder, who does not suffer fools easily. Someone must have become really fed up with her because one misty morning a few hundred yards down the beach from the famed Hotel Del Coronado, Shirley's lifeless body, her head bashed in with a blunt instrument, is discovered by joggers. This after she'd been seen lunching with George Raft; hobnobbing with up and coming actor, Vic Steele; angrily ignoring fellow journalist Hank Kendall; exchanging jealous looks with hair stylist Evie MacPherson; and making a general nuisance of herself everywhere she turned. United Artists is aghast and so is Joe This murder has to be solved and removed from the front pages of America's newspapers as soon as possible or when it's released, this picture will be known as 'the murder movie', hardly a selling point for a rollicking comedy.

Book Fourteen—1960
DEAD MEN PAY NO DEBTS

Among the hard and fast rules in Joe
Bernardi's life is this one:
Do not, under any circumstances, travel
east during the winter months. In this way
one avoids dealing with snow, ice, sleet,
frostbite and pneumonia. Unfortunately he
has had to break this rule and having done
so, is paying the price. His novel 'A Family
of Strangers' has been optioned for a major motion picture and he
needs to fly east in January to meet with the talented director who
has taken the option. Stuart Rosenberg, in the midst of directing
"Murder Inc." an expose of the 1930's gang of killers for hire,
has insisted Joe write the screenplay and he needs several days to
guide Joe in the right direction. Reluctantly Joe agrees, a decision
which he will quickly rue when he finds himself up to his belly
button with drug dealers, loan sharks, Mafia hit men, wannabe
Broadway stars and an up and coming New York actor named
Peter Falk who may be on the verge of stardom. Someone has
beaten drug dealer Gino Finucci to death and left his body in the
basement of The Mudhole, an off-off-Broadway theater which is
home to Amythyst Breen, a one time darling of Broadway struggling to find her way back to the top and also Jonathan Harker,
slimy and ambitious, an actor caught in the grip of drug addiction
even as he struggles to get that one lucky break that will propel
him to stardom. Even as Joe fights to remain above the fray, he
can feel himself being inexorably drawn into the intrigue of under-
world vendettas culminating in a face to face confrontation with
Carlo Gambino, the boss of bosses, and the most powerful Mafia
chieftain in New York City.

Book Fifteen—1961
APPLE ANNIE AND THE DUDE

Joe Bernardi is a sucker for a sad story and especially when it comes from an old pal like Lila James who, after years of trying, has landed a plum assignment as a movie publicist. Frank Capra has okayed her for his newest film, A Pocketful of Miracles, now shooting on the Paramount lot. Get this right and her little company has a big future which is when God intervenes by inflicting her with a broken leg which will put her out of commission for at least a couple of weeks. Enter Joe as Sir Galahad to save the day and fill in. A simple favor, you say? Not so fast. First he'll have to deal with Heather Leeds, Lila's assistant, an ambitious tart in the mold of Eve Harrington, a devious cupcake who makes enemies the way Betty Crocker makes biscuits. Making his job even more difficult are the on-set feuds between Bette Davis and Glenn Ford with Capra getting migraines trying to referee. And then the fun really starts as a mysterious woman named Claire Philby from Northwestern University shows up to give Heather an award and maybe something else she never bargained for. Who killed Heather Leeds? Was it Philby or maybe Heather's husband Buddy Lovejoy, a struggling television writer, or perhaps even his writing partner, Seth Donnelley. And what about Heather's ex-husband Travis Wright who was just released from prison and claims Heather owes him $9,000,000 which he left in her care? Of more concern to Joe is the shadow of suspicion that has fallen on Dexter Craven, an old friend from the Warner Bros. days. Good old Lila, she's lying peacefully in a hospital bed while Joe deals with a nest of vipers, one of which is a cold blooded killer, and a movie in the making which is being tattered by conflicting egos. It's enough to make a man long for happier days when he was slogging through muddy France at the tail-end of World War II.

Book Sixteen—1962
'TILL DEATH US DO PART

Who would want to kill a sweet old guy like Mike O'Malley, the prop master on Universal's "To Kill a Mockingbird"? Nobody, but dead he is, the victim of a hit and run that looks more like deliberate murder than accidental death. More likely the killer was after Mike's grandson Rory who had earned the enmity of Hank Greb, a burly mean-spirited teamster as well as Wayne Daniels, a wannabe actor, who claims erroneously that Rory's carelessness caused his face to be disfigured. Is this any of Joe Bernardi's business? Not really but when he showed up on the Mockingbird set as a favor to his hospitalized partner, Bertha Bowles, to woo newcomer William Windom to join the Bowles & Bernardi management firm, Joe was sucked into the situation right up to his tonsils, something he had little time for since his first priority was handling publicity for 'Lilies of the Field', a Sidney Poitier film, shooting in Tucson. Meanwhile Joe, who longs to write a second novel, has become increasingly bored with working at movie promotion and publicity. A twist of fate finds him befriended by Truman Capote and by Harper Lee who, like Joe, is trying to find that elusive second novel. Both are huge admirers of Joe's highly praised first novel and vow to help Joe get it made as a motion picture, even as Joe tries to expose the truth about Mike O'Malleys' death.

Book Eighteen—1964
MURDER ABOARD THE HIGHLAND ROSE

The night was dark. Clouds obscured the moon. The elaborate yacht owned by Joseph Kennedy lay at anchor in Monterey Bay. Shortly past midnight a shot rang out. A man aboard the yacht had been murdered. The police ferried out to the boat and found nothing amiss and the next morning Kennedy's 'Highland Rose' continued its journey north to San Francisco. Rumors abounded and for thirty-five years the events of that night in 1929 have been hidden in mystery. And now it is 1964 and it has fallen to Joe Bernardi to solve the mystery and write the book that tells the truth about that terrible night. The rumored victim, an obscure talent agent named Archie Farrell. The rumored murderer, Joseph P. Kennedy himself. Witnesses to the rumored killing, film stars Gloria Swanson and Gladys George, writer Frances Marion, and producer Edward Albee, among others. And why, after thirty-five years, has the solution to this killing become so important? Because 1964 is an election year and John F. Kennedy will be running again for the Presidency. Will he succeed? There are those who hope he will not and they are working on a hatchet job, an expose of Joe Kennedy as a philanderer and a killer showing the President to be the seed of evil. Deadly forces array themselves against Joe in his quest for truth. It appears that the secret of the Highland Rose must be kept hidden at all costs while the fate of the country hangs in the balance.

Book Nineteen—1965
ASHES TO ASHES

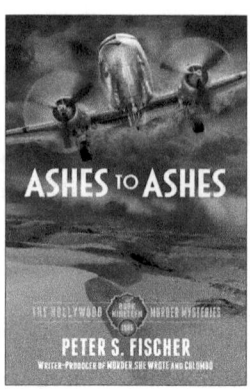

His name is Armitage McLeod but he is better known in the business as Anonymous Army. That's because he toils in the shadows, highly talented and well paid but none of his best movies lists his name as a screenwriter. He is a script doctor, caring little for credit. Every major studio has used him over and over again and he always delivers. He is also one of Joe Bernardi's oldest and dearest friends, a man who literally saved Joe's life on more than one occasion. And so when the phone rang in his office, Joe listened panic-stricken as Army reached out in a garbled plea for help that abruptly ended in mid-sentence. It took Joe two days to find out where Army was calling from and when he did he hopped the next available plane to Yuma, Arizona, where they were shooting a Jimmy Stewart survival picture called 'The Flight of the Phoenix'. When he arrived, he found that Army was among the missing, having disappeared without a trace throwing the production into turmoil. Despite what most directors believe, a production without a talented writer standing by for emergencies, is a production in deep trouble. Thus began a search for his old friend which suddenly threw Joe into the middle of a drug war between notorious mobster Mickey Cohen and the Crips, a bloodthirsty black gang spawned by the L.A. ghettos. His attempts to find his old friend are stymied at every turn by a bigoted chief of police and when the body of an attractive young woman is found in the desert close by the film location, Joe finds himself having to answer for a lot more than curiosity.

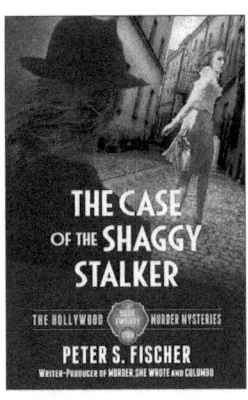

Book Twenty–1965
THE CASE OF THE SHAGGY STALKER

Once again there's a chance that the first Sam August film will be made because handsome and virile leading man Robert Wagner is interested. Joe Bernardi, the fertile brain behind this literary super spy, can't wait to pin Wagner down to a contract, but when he visits the set of Paul Newman's newest film, 'Harper", in which Wagner co-stars, strange circumstances pop into view. Why is Wagner's newest stand-in being introduced to him as Ben Boxer when Joe knows perfectly well that Boxer's real name is Gunnar Larsen, the number one guy in private investigator Cosmo Stryker's stable of operatives. And why can't he get straight answers to simple questions? What does Wagner need to hide? A great deal, it turns out. A schlock novelist from his wife Marian's past has turned up and is scaring the devil out of the entire family. Notifying the police is only asking for unwanted publicity, hence the services of Cosmo Stryker. But when the novelist, Horatio Cummings, is murdered in a back alley, the circumstances clumsily arranged to look like a mugging gone bad, Wagner suddenly becomes suspect number one. Luckily there exist suspects number two, three and four, etc. For example a five foot tall Cockney femme fatale and her Irish lawyer or the on-the-cheap B Movie producer Garrison King or lumbering Tough Tony Trippi, once a hero on Omaha Beach, now one of the most feared loan sharks in the city. And what's all this have to do with a woman who lays dying in a hospice in Belfast, Northern Ireland? Joe is going to have to do a lot of unraveling to get Wagner out of hot water and into his cherished movie.

FUTURE TITLES IN THE SERIES:

Warner's Last Stand